Russian Poker

By R.L. Murphy

R.L. Murphy

Visit my website at www.rlmurphy.net

Edited by S. Ryan and Ashley B.

Printed in the United States of America

First Printing: April 2012

ISBN-13 978-0-6156377-0-9

I would like to thank everyone that has supported me in my writing. Except for you. You know who you are.

I'd like to double thank everyone who has given me feedback, good and bad. Except for you. You know who you are.

I'd like to triple thank my daughter Iris for being the flower in my life that does nothing but bloom and shine. Especially you, and I make sure to tell you how special you are and what you mean to me.

R.L. Murphy

Prologue

Steven Jones spent the majority of his time sitting on his bed in his cell on death row after being convicted of killing his wife and four year old daughter.

He stared through the glass barrier, out into the maximum security cell across from his own. Another death row inmate had been there for the past six months. Before that, Steven had no one to watch. He didn't know the inmate's name from across the corridor, or even what the man had done, but the inmate intrigued him. The inmate across the corridor was white, bald and frail, and reminded Steven of the musician Moby. The inmate always sat on his cell floor in the yoga lotus position, and was always reading. The only things in the inmate's cell were an ever changing stack of books, and a purple flower by his bed.

Steven felt like an outcast in a building filled with outcasts. He was in his mid thirties, with short, brown hair, and brown eyes. Since Steven was twenty years old, he had been mistaken for Charlie Sheen, and often partied like him too. Steven had a friend that was in prison once, but never dreamed it would be him locked up. His friend told him how easy it was to bribe guards to get alcohol. His friend, however, wasn't in a Texas maximum security penitentiary. The only other person Steven saw during the week was The Tall Guard. He visited him four times daily: once at six for breakfast, noon for lunch, again at two for exercise, and again at five for dinner. When it was time for sleep, The Tall Guard would yell from down the corridor. Steven was on the opposite end, but he still looked forward to hearing The Tall Guard's voice. During the weekdays, this was Steven's only form of human contact.

The weekends were a different story though. A shorter guard worked on the weekends. He was also the same man who took Steven Jones from the court room to his cell when he was sentenced. The Short Guard was also a genuinely good guy, unlike The Tall Guard. He would keep him updated on all the updates in the UFC. Today was Saturday. Steven knew The Short Guard should be there for lunch. Saturday was Steven's favorite day because it meant it was turkey sandwich day. He never liked turkey very much but it was his daughter, Sarah's, favorite.

"Wake up, asshole!" the Tall Guard said as he pounded on the glass barrier with his baton. Steven was surprised to see him. It wasn't The Tall Guard's day to work and he didn't have any lunch with him. No lunch meant no turkey sandwich, and no turkey sandwich meant no reminiscing about Sarah. "C'mon, get your ass up! We're going for a trip."

"What for? It's not exercise hour yet, is it?" Steven asked, "Is it time for my physical already? You guys springing for Flu shots this year?"

"Yeah, shots...let's go with that," The Tall Guard said.

Steven pressed his back flatly against the glass barrier. Both of his hands slipped through the small flap where his turkey sandwich should have been. The Tall Guard wrapped his handcuffs around Steven's wrists and tightly locked them. The Tall Guard never had a problem with Steven, which was rare for death row inmates, they usually disregard the rules due to having nothing to lose. The Tall Guard unlocked the door and told Steven to turn around. He complied.

"Walk in front of me," The Tall Guard said.

"What, why? Where are we going?"

"I said walk, not talk. I'll tell *you* what to do," The Tall Guard said pressing his baton across the nape of Steven's neck. The sensation gave Steven chills. They continued to walk for twenty feet, passing a dozen maximum security cells. "I never get to go this way when I go out for exercise," Steven thought to himself. An inmate pounded on the glass barrier between himself and Steven. He licked the glass as Steven walked passed. "Turn left," The Tall Guard instructed. Steven had a bad feeling he knew where they were going. This hallway only had two doors. The lethal injection room was on the right, and on the left was solitary confinement. Steven's steps became more reluctant. Steven was hoping for left.

"I guess the rumors are true then?" Steven asked.

"About what?" The Tall Guard answered. The Tall Guard knew what Steven was referring too. Steven could feel the Tall

Guard sneer.

"About the death penalty. You know, about it being illegal, and each state having to decide what to do with the rest of the death row inmates?" Steven asked.

"Yup, sure is. We got thirty days from yesterday to decide what to do with you assholes. Can you believe it? It only took the great state of Texas twelve hours to decide what to do with you vagabonds," The Tall Guard gloated as if he had some say in the decision. Steven could feel the sadistic grin coming from The Tall Guard behind him.

"What took 'em so long?" Steven asked, returning the grin.

"That's what I thought too." The Tall guard stopped Steven in front of the door to the execution room. The Tall Guard unlocked the door from his huge metal ring of keys. The Tall Guard took the handcuffs off Steven's wrists and instructed Steven to open the door. Steven entered the room. "Just have a seat in the chair that is assigned to you. We'll be back. You'll know which one is yours." Steven didn't know what he meant by "we" and didn't like the sound of it.

The lethal injection room was completely gutted. There was only a large, oval, metal table, and ten metal chairs with crudely written paper signs written in black marker attached with duct tape onto their backs. In the room was a two-way mirror where the observation room obviously was for spectators to witness the end of a monster's life safely. Steven circled around the table looking for "his" chair, the chair with the label that they thought fit him. After checking the first nine signs without any luck, he spotted the label "Child Murderer" on the tenth chair. Steven took the label off the chair, crumpled it, and threw it in the corner of the room. It wasn't because he didn't want anyone else to see it. It was because the label wasn't true. Steven Jones was innocent.

Russian Poker

The Innocent heard The Short Guard talking to someone outside the execution room. Soon after, the door opened. A Middle Eastern man with long stringy black hair entered. He appeared to be in his late thirties. "He doesn't look like a terrorist," the Innocent thought, "but in this world, who could tell?" The Middle Eastern man found his seat next to Steven's. His seat was labeled "The Terrorist". The Terrorist sat down in his assigned chair and spat on the ground in front of The Innocent. The Innocent shook his head in disgust at The Terrorist's sign of disrespect. Upon closer look, The Terrorist was a clean-shaven man and not bad looking. "He doesn't look like a bad guy," The Innocent thought to himself, "but if he is not then why would he be here? Then again, why am I here?" He continued to maintain his innocence.

The Innocent peered at The Terrorist with disgust. "I want to punch him in his camel fucking face," he thought to himself. He resisted the urge, and said nothing. A few minutes passed. The Innocent heard a booming voice from far away. As it got closer, he could tell that it was a black man's voice. The door opened.

"Those punk motherfuckers need to calm their asses down before they catch an ass beatin'. They think I won't do it?

Shiiiiit! I'll spend a month in the hole for the chance to crack that mother fucka!" The Terrorist looked at the black man with almost as much utter contempt as The Innocent. The Innocent wondered what kind of anti-American blasphemy was going through the mind of The Terrorist. The black man found a chair labeled "The Gangster" and sat down at the table. "I guess that's all I am to these motherfuckers! All I is, is some sorta gangsta to 'em? It's because I'm black, right? That's it innit?" The Innocent got a better look at the black man. He wasn't what The Innocent expected. The Gangster is in his early 40's, dressed casually in a polo shirt and jeans. He noticed that the Gangster took the time to prepare himself. The Gangster's short, thick, black hair looked like he shaved himself with immaculate precision.

The Terrorist saw that the guards were sending them in counter clock-wise. "How cute," he thought to himself.

The Innocent couldn't believe who he saw walking through the door. He had heard that he was kept on the same cell block as himself, but no one ever saw him. The Prairie Dog Killer was one of the most notorious serial killers in modern history. He was caught only after killing an untold amount of women over thirteen years. To this day, no one knew exactly how many lives he took, and dumped into the river, but they projected around thirty. The Prairie Dog Killer admitted only to the one the authorities saw him commit. "Clear the way, celebrity coming through!" The Prairie Dog Killer said as he walked around the table. He found his seat

While The Serial Killer was still ranting the door opened again. The four inmates turned their heads to look at who was entering the room. "You've got to be shitting me," The Innocent said barely audibly. He thought this freak had to be in his mid-twenties at most. The Innocent noticed the two foot tall Mohawk the freak wore, and the piercings in his face, ears, and nose. The Innocent thought that this freak was probably an asshole.

"Something catch your eye?" The freak asked the Terrorist.

"You're a disgrace to your family," The Terrorist replied.

"Oooohhh, real harsh man, real harsh," The Gangster was cracking himself up. The Innocent snickered too. The freak sat down in the chair labeled "The Hitman."

Another black man came through the execution room's door. Though his skin color was the only similarity to The Gangster. He was a tremendously obese man, dressed in a black suit with a tie. The Innocent wondered, "Where do guys that large buy suits?"

"I bet this guy hasn't seen his dick since the Gulf War," The Serial Killer said to no one in particular.

"What the hell is this guy doing here?" There was no happiness in the sunken eyes of the obese black man, leaving the inmates to think that his humanity had left him a long time ago. The Innocent thought, "He probably got tired of his wife nagging him all the time, and one night strangled her for blocking Monday Night Football." He sat down in the seat labeled "The Preacher," his body spilling over the sides of his chair as it creaked.

The door opened again. Everyone eagerly anticipated the next inmate as they heard a voice they hadn't heard in a long time. A woman walked through the door to the delight of the inmates. The bruising on her wrists made it obvious to the inmates that she had been struggling with the guards. The guards had taken her shoes and left her barefoot. There was a crazy look in her eyes, the kind of look only a woman having survived sexual abuse in her childhood would have. Even noticing this The Innocent is attracted to her still. Everyone could tell she was a heavy drug user just by the toll it had taken on her face. The Innocent saw women like her on his way in to work every day. Best he could guess, she probably killed her family in a meth-induced rage.

"You rarely see such a group of social fuck-ups in one place," The Innocent thought. He was amazed by it actually. He almost wanted a bowl of popcorn, just to see what kind of sideshow would come fumbling in next. The Woman sat down in her chair labeled "The Hooker" which happened to be directly across from The Innocent. The Innocent thought "She'll probably spend a lot of time looking directly at me, lucky."

Two more inmates came in at the same time. One inmate looked like a geek, the kind of guy you would expect to be jerking off to Internet pornography in his mother's basement on a Saturday night. He was not ugly, but he wasn't attractive either. He was the kind of guy that no one told how to take care of himself. He was wearing a black shirt with a reference to Doctor Who on it and jean shorts. He looked like someone that needed nothing more than a little self confidence to be successful in life. The Innocent thought he probably had a jock father who was disappointed by his son every day. He sits down in "The Geek" chair slouched over with horrific posture.

The other inmate who entered with The Geek was clearly not sane. In his mid-thirties, he had the unmistakable look of insanity, the kind no one could ever fake. His eyes told it all. Chills crept down The Innocent's spine as the insane man made eye contact with him. The Innocent was afraid of him, as was The Woman. The inmate was escorted by the Short Guard to the chair labeled "The Cannibal." The Cannibal quickly scanned the room, as if he was looking for someone in particular. The more he looked, the happier he seemed to be. The Cannibal made eye contact one by one with each inmate in the room and started clapping his hands excitedly, and talking to himself.

The only vacant chair left happened to be the chair

directly to the left of The Innocent. The Innocent thought to himself "This whole ordeal seems like they had planned on doing it for years. Like someone thinking of survival plans in case zombies rise out of the ground, just to be surprised the day it actually happens." The last man came in without saying a word. It was the man who The Innocent spent a lot of time observing in the cell across fromhim.

The Innocent's first thought was that he had never seen anyone whiter in his life. The Innocent thought the inmate looked like a guy who acts smarter than everyone else, all because he listens to Radio Head, or he "gets" foreign films. The inmate's head was clean-shaven as usual, but the Innocent noticed all of the little bumps and dips in his head. You can never see those from afar. He sat down gracefully into the chair labeled "The Pacifist" in lotus position as if he had been practicing for this moment.

The Tall Guard closed the door behind him as he entered. The Innocent saw the gun strapped to his back, but he also saw another pistol in The Tall Guard's hand. "Okay shitheads, here's the plan. The Warden had to decide what to do with all of you, and him being gracious and all, he decided to let one of you guys out free and clear of all charges. But he's not giving it to you. No, you're going have to earn it," The Tall Guard said.

"Earn it how?" The Woman asked eagerly.

"Glad you asked, sweet tits. Here's the plan. You guys ever see that movie with Christopher Walken where he has to play Russian roulette with Robert De Niro?" The Tall Guard asked. No one answered.

The Tall Guard sighed. "We're going to play a game. We have a gun here that holds six bullets. In every round, one person is going to get this gun. Whoever has the gun has to shoot someone *else* in the room. You get one squeeze of the trigger then you pass the gun to the next person. The next person puts another bullet in the chamber, and rise and repeat until the gun goes off into someone's skull. Once it goes off, the rest of the bullets in the chamber are emptied, and we drag the unlucky sack of shit out of the room. Then we do it all over again. We stop only when there's one asshole left, and that asshole gets to go free. How does that sound?"

"Sounds like my average Saturday night, Hoss," The Serial Killer said. The Tall Guard ignored his remark.

"If you pull the trigger more than once per round, we kill you. If you load more than one bullet in the chamber each round, we kill you. If you take the gun out of turn, we kill you. If you stand up out of your seat for more than thirty seconds, we kill you. If you try to shoot one of us while in the room, we kill you. Once the buzzer goes off, you have two minutes to pull the trigger. If you do not, we kill you. If you are the last fucker alive in this room, we will *not* kill you," The Tall Guard explained. "Any questions?"

The Innocent thought, "If they want me to play their silly fucking game for a chance out of here, I'm game." He would do it for Sarah. "Only for you," he whispered to himself.

The Short Guard walked to the table and placed the gun and a box of bullets on the table. "You're first," The Short Guard said as he emptied the box of bullets onto the table, clanking on the metal surface. "Just remember, you pull the trigger once. The gun is to be passed clockwise. And don't forget to empty the remaining bullets out after it goes off or..."

"Let me guess, you'll kill us," The Innocent interrupted.

"Yeah, we kill you," The Short Guard said. He left the room leaving the inmates with the echo of the door as he locked them into their fate.

"Well folks, if there's no questions we will leave you to it. Enjoy your game of Russian Poker."

The Innocent

The cool feel of steel against his hand made The Innocent anxious. He nervously placed a bullet in the chamber of the gun. Even though the courts believed otherwise, he had never held a gun before. He was innocent, at least innocent of the two counts of first degree murder that he was accused of. He was accused of coming home from work and shooting his wife, her heart exploding like an M80 in her chest. Then twelve of his peers said that he went upstairs in his own home and shot his daughter Sarah in the head, leaving brain chunks on the curtains. He never thought of himself as a saint, but he knew he wasn't a whack job killer either. They had arguments that got a little harsh from time to time, but what marriage didn't?

He probably shouldn't have been drinking as much as he had, but that didn't make him a killer. He worked as a hotel manager in Dallas. It was nothing fancy, just a small place that rented out to businessmen stopping in for the night. The Innocent always found it funny that there wasn't a cash register, just a box for the patrons to drop their money into when they needed shaving supplies or condoms. Now his job consisted of staying alive and catching up on all the books his teachers in high school said were the classics. He thought whoever said Mark Twain was good should be in here instead of him.

he was in the execution room facing his fate with nine

other social fuck-ups that had actually done this before. If he wanted to get out alive, he'd have to be like them. None of them deserve the prize, they're all guilty. You can see can see it in their eyes.

They've murdered a human being before. "Fucking scumbags," The Innocent thought. "If I follow through with this, am I any better than them? What does it matter? If I don't, I'll just die innocent. No one believes me anyway. There's nothing more terrible than looking into the eyes of everyone you love and knowing that they think you killed your family. Seeing their disgust, their hatred, and their utter contempt for you is unspeakable. I may as well play the part of the killer. This is about survival. I may not want it as much as some of these fucks, but I do deserve it. Why shouldn't I get what I deserve? So should they. The more of these fuckers I take out, the better my chances are. I see nothing but hardened faces around this table. But who am I to judge who should go first?"

He didn't think he could do this. He hoped the gun wouldn't go off. The Innocent needed to make his decision of who he was going to shoot. His wife would want him to take out the worst person, but he didn't know what any of these guys had done except for The Prairie Dog Killer. He wondered if he could live with himself if the gun went off. Would his eyes change the same way theirs had?

They said you could always look into someone's eyes to

see what they'd done. His mind was reeling with questions. "Why should I let one of these filthy motherfuckers kill me? Why give them that joy? Should I just kill myself? Why put myself through this shit when I already know my ass is toast? I don't have a life to go back to even if I did make it out of here. My wife. My fucking wife and child are gone. Even if I get out of here alive, I'll never be able to hold them again," The Innocent thought to himself. "Society thinks I destroyed the only thing precious to me, my little Sarah. I promised you I wouldn't let anyone hurt you. I lied, and I'm sorry. I'm even sorrier that I couldn't find the cocksucker who did this to you. Please forgive me, Sarah."

He caught himself starting to tear up, a natural reaction when he thought about his daughter. He needed to gather himself. The Innocent knew if he started crying in front of the inmates, they would think him weak. He didn't want to become an easy target for someone else. He told himself to act tough, and not to take any shit from these sociopaths. "Be a man," He said to himself, "be a man."

The buzzer went off. He was ready but was breathing erratically. He only had two minutes to decide who he was going to shoot. He just wanted to get it over with. He prayed the gun wouldn't go off. The Innocent lifted the gun off the table and pointed it at the kid with the tattoos spiraling around his neck.

The Innocent joked to himself that the kid probably had more metal in his face than the gun that he was about to kill him with. He made his decision. He's the one The Innocent deemed the biggest scumbag in this room. For a second he felt like God. He was easily the youngest person here, but still got to live a dozen times longer than Sarah. The Innocent lifted his arm and fully extend it toward the kid. The Hitman smiled, a grin like rusty nails, his teeth having rotted out of his mouth. It turned The Innocent's stomach. "It has to be from drug use, fucking crank addict I bet," The Innocent guessed. "He is just a depressed fuck that must want to die." He didn't want to kill him though. He heard the black guy mumbling something. The Innocent glanced over and saw the black guy laughing at him. He saw what they were both snickering about. It was his own hand. It was shaking uncontrollably.

"Is that spooky sucka' scaring you, bitch?" The Gangster mocked him.

"That cock sucker!" The Innocent thought. He couldn't help his face from showing exactly how he felt. "It's fuckers like you who deserve to die! Fucker running his mouth at times like this! No fucking respect. Blacks don't know when to shut their mouths, always so fucking rude." The Innocent slowly and carefully swivels his stiffened arm, aiming the gun between the eyes of The Gangster. "You're not talking now, are ya?" He was almost four feet away from the Innocent. The Gangster was still trying to play it cool, play it like he didn't care. "So fucking insecure! Anytime they are not in control, they have to act like they don't give a shit," The Innocent said. He wanted the Gangster to fear *him* for once. The Gangster deserved to fear death. "It won't go off, but maybe for a second he'll fear me." He said barely audible. The Innocent tightened his grip on the gun. He looked The Gangster dead in the eyes and said,

"Fuck you, gutter monkey!"

He had always wanted to say that. The way he said it was obviously upsetting. *He* feared *him* now. He thought The Innocent hated him for being black. No, The Innocent hated him for not caring. Like a small child hiding from the boogie man, The Innocent closed his eyes and pulled the trigger. It gave some resistance. As he pulled the trigger back all the way back, all he could think is...please let me stay innocent.

Russian Poker

Russian Poker

R.L. Murphy

-Click-

The Pacifist

The Innocent relieved, handed the gun to the next man, the Pacifist. As he was given the gun The Pacifist thought to himself, "Ten minutes. What a waste of time. They know I'm a pacifist. After the accident, I swore to never hurt another soul. I'm just going to sit here at peace with myself. I wonder what they think I'm going to do."

He heard a few whispers from across the table. "I will stay in lotus position in my chair meditating. The longer I try to center myself, the faster the time goes. There is all this negative energy in the room. It's not hard to sense the dirty souls around me. I know I'm no different. They never made peace with themselves. Even if they did apologize to the victim's families, it wouldn't be sincere. They don't have any remorse in them. It really is a pity. They will never realize this *is* justice. Karma is the unspoken justice felt by all."   He opened his eyes. They were staring at him like he was an overturned school bus. "You can relax. I've already made my decision," he said trying to sooth his fellow inmates. It was important that he try to calm them down.

"It's me, isn't it? You're going to shoot me because I called him a monkey. I, I, I can explain," The Innocent stuttered.

"You need not worry., that part of my life is behind me,"

The Pacifist interrupted him.

"Lemme guess. You're innocent, right?" The Gangster joked.

"Just because I made peace with myself for my actions, doesn't mean I am clean or innocent. I'm guilty," The Pacifist confessed.

"Aw man, I knew you were one of those new-age Christian faggots," The Serial Killer replied.

"Religion can only provide forgiveness and false security. I have made peace with myself. I no longer fear consequences. Free your mind. Quit seeking forgiveness from those you cannot see. Discover yourself, the only one that is truly close to you," The Pacifist stated. The Gangster snickered as if he was told a crude, yet unfunny, joke.

"Isn't it a bit too late for all that 'self awareness' bullshit?" questioned the man two chairs to The Pacifist's left. He was a tall, gangly, but clean-cut man who appeared to be a highly intelligent, angry, passive-aggressive geek. The Pacifist shrugged. "It seems illogical to seek internal answers. Considering we're all killers, why accept self truths from the morally bankrupt?" He peered into the eyes of everyone around the table.

"We all have reasons why we took the actions we did. Just because this country has deemed it illegal doesn't make it immoral. Morals are relative." The buzzer went off. The Pacifist knew he was running out of time to convince them. "Follow my lead, even if they kill us for it!" He picked up the gun with his left hand. The Pacifist hadn't touched one since that night. "Don't commit even more havoc, don't play by their system. If I don't shoot, the guards will kill me. They never said I had to aim *at* anyone!" He closed his eyes, centered himself, and slid the trigger back.

-Click-

The Cannibal

The bullet ricocheted off the ceiling and landed near the door. The Pacifist slid the gun over to the next inmate. The Cannibal placed another bullet in the chamber hungrily. It was obvious that everyone in the room was scared of him. He didn't have the sanity to completely think to himself. Instead he muttered under his breath, "I can't believe this. I'm so happy! Ten minutes. Ten minutes until I get my chance! They wouldn't let me do this unless they wanted me to feed. It's been so long. It's been so long since I tasted flesh. Biting my lip secretly and sucking the drops of blood has been my only taste for it in years," The Cannibal thought. "They haven't let me near anyone since the accident."

"Why don't they understand my blood is drying? I need it to survive. I'm not crazy. I just know what I need. The thought of all the blood in my veins drying makes me nervous. I can't think of a worse way to die. I must feed. I've been feeding for as long as I can remember," The Cannibal said.

"I'm 42 years old. Nine minutes left. They think I'm dumb. I'm not though. I went to college. They didn't understand my disease either. I never meant to kill anyone. Why would I? The longer they live, the more blood they make. That's the blood I need to live. Skin grows back too. The organs don't though. How good the organs are though. The satisfying toughness of biting into a fresh ripped heart is unmistakable. Its hard exterior makes you bite hard into it. When you do, the teeth sink into it like a ripe plum. I'll never forget the first bladder I ever tasted. Silly me, I never made the connection. It's so bitter. Such a mess. I just told my dorm mates I pissed myself. It's not my fault...it's his!" The Cannibal thought to himself.

The rest of room sat in silence as The Cannibal continued his rant. "I think the one who gave him the disease is to blame. The skinhead, he cursed me. I think he has the power of the dragon. Dragons have strong magic. Eight minutes 45 seconds left. It's Strong enough to slowly dry a person's blood. People like dragons. I fear them. Seven minutes left. I don't like guns, never used one. I never needed one. The aiming is not as precise as they would make you think. Too much wasted blood. It's for cowards who don't know any better.

I guess I better decide who I want. I get choices again. The best moments of my life was deciding who I thought out of millions of people in the Austin area I would taste. I get choices again! I'm not settling for rats anymore. After this, I'll get more. There are plenty of people here. They'll understand. It's a medical condition, they have to accommodate me. How about the woman? She's so sexy. I want to bite into her inner thigh, and look up at her as I lick the blood the blood flowing down her calf," The Cannibal thought to himself.

"There's a black man not four feet away. I've never had the pleasure. Wonder what it's like? Maybe their blood is stronger. It's stronger from all the years of slavery. Stronger body equals a stronger soul. Maybe it'll hold longer than the normal white blood I've been used to. To get to it I'll need to go through two people. There's the pudgy man to my left in the glasses, as well as that beautiful woman. Even if I only get ten minutes to finish, it'll be enough to hold me over till I get to him. They say period blood is better for the body since it's fresh. I hope it's true. They also said that about baby blood. They lied. I even followed the directions exactly as they told me. Baby blood was supposed to be pure and innocent. They lied. Six minutes left. Good thing I didn't let it go to waste. Since it was a newborn everything was so soft. Even the heavy bone snapped in half. It was the best I ever had, but they lied to me. Five minutes left. In 300 seconds I have a 50 percent chance of saving myself, and inching my way closer to the cure. The cure for my disease is flowing inside my veins," The Cannibal rambled to himself.

"Eight of you can relax, I've made my decision," he said. The Cannibal said glancing around the room. "I need to cure my disease, and they have told me that this man is the only cure," he matter-of-factly said pointing directly to the older black man.

"What the hell are you talking about?" The Gangster said perplexed.

"I'm sick! Diseased! Nothing can cure it unless I feed it! It's nothing personal. I don't care if I make it out of here as long as I get cured! I'm going to drink you're blood! I'm diseased! You fuckers can't rob me of this! Anyone who gets in my way I will devour! The dragons curse will be broken. I will get my revenge on the Arian Brotherhood!" The Cannibal said.

"Man, calm the fuck down," The Geek said after what the Cannibal believed to be truth. Tears start coming out of the Cannibals eyes out of frustration.

"They don't understand! They don't believe me. They don't think I'm sick! I'm not crazy!" He tried to convince them. He had to make them understand.

"Yeah, you're bat-shit insane buddy" insulted The Innocent which by now had been labeled the racist of the group.

"I can't wait to lick your essence off the barrel of this gun!" He slams the gun on the table in frustration. "You just want out to kill again mindlessly. You kill out of personal gain, I do it to *live*," he said tears gathering in his eyes. The moment he had been waiting for, the buzzer went off. He told himself that The Geek next to him didn't matter. He needed to feed on him. This would mean he would try for the middle aged black man next. As if he needed directions to his cure, which stops he needed to make.

"Three bullets, three blanks. The Dragon is with me." The Cannibal murmured. The gun is lighter than he thought it would be. He grinned. "My brain is tainted, and I wouldn't want to let his poison inside me," he said and aimed at The Geek's balding forehead. "I prepare to feast. I like them alive while I start consuming them, but I'll make exceptions," he said. The Cannibal squeezed the trigger, salivating, waiting for the answer that the gun is about to give him. As he pulls it back he gets his answer.

-Bang-

The Story of Roger Pain

"How many must I kill for you to love me?"

Great, another day where I wake up five minutes before my alarm does. I shut it off and pick up the slacks off the floor that I've been wearing all week. At least it's Friday and I can spend most of the weekend by myself playing World of Warcraft.

I grab a shirt and tie out of my closet, put it on and tie the tie in a full Windsor knot. I go to my bathroom and brush my teeth. How often am I supposed to change the heads on an electric toothbrush? I spray my neck twice with my favorite cologne, Green Irish Tweed by Creed. Very few people appreciate the elegance of high class cologne. Most people are happy with their swill of cheap inferior chemicals and I'll never understand it. I go downstairs and I find my dress socks in the same place as I do every day, under my coffee table next to my shoes. It's the one bad habit I allow myself. I put them on and walk out of my house.

I lock my front door and open the garage door. I get inside my new Toyota Corolla and drive to work. Another useless day to my useless job where my useless boss does half the work and makes twice as much money. They can't take my commute away from me. No matter what I can sing whatever song I want on my way to work and no one can hear, no one can judge, no one can tell me no. Never has anyone told me I wasn't good enough here, never any rejection. I change it to Possum Kingdom by The Toadies, my favorite. I pull into the parking garage as the song ends its third play.

I step into the large corporate skyscraper's revolving door. I scan my ID badge at the security check point and say good morning to the security guard. He doesn't even look up. I reach the elevator and push the button and wait. I hear two women talk about how one of them had a big interview and thinks she nailed it. Stupid bitch. My elevator opens and the two women cut in front of me to get on first. I go in and it closes behind me. They keep talking about how much she thinks the pay increase is going to be, and it makes me want to vomit. It's always them, it's never me. No matter how hard I work or how much money I save the company they never care. It's never me.

The door opens at the twelfth floor and I get off. I walk through the rows and rows of cubicles until I get to mine, the one by the window. I may hate everything I do at my job, and everything this business stands for, but they can't take away my window.

The view out of it overlooks the park where happy people walk their dogs and jog. I log onto my computer and start up my programs. My boss, that dumb bastard leans over my desk with his usual coffee cup full of whatever swill they pass as coffee in the break room.

"Hey you know that report you sent me Tuesday? Apparently there was a problem with the formatting of the spreadsheet," He said as he puts down his coffee on my desk and adjusts his tie.

"The spreadsheet is fine, I made it. Who did it go to, Thomas? I'll reformat it so even he can understand it. Is that all Mr. West?" I say as he lifts his coffee from my desk, leaving a ring of the dark liquid.

"Yeah that's all I ask Roger, is do it right the first time," Mr. West said walking away from my cubicle. Stupid asshole didn't even hear what I said. Thomas shouldn't even have that job. I have no idea what he did or said to get that promotion over me, but I know it couldn't have made sense. I reformat the sheet and email it back to Thomas directly.

I grab my water bottle and head to the break room. I squeeze past the obese woman from accounts receivable trying to decide what she wants out of the vending machine to make her even fatter as I make my way to the water dispenser. As my bottle is half way full, I smell it.

I smell the scent that makes me get out of bed every morning, Tara Redding. She was hired into the company the same day as me six years ago. I sat next to her in training and her perfume drove me wild that first week and hasn't stopped since. I went to a department store smelling dozens of bottles before finding the one that she wore every day. It's Burberry Brit. The day I noticed she wasn't wearing it anymore I bought her a new bottle.

"H-Hey Tara how are you doing?" I asked.

"Oh hey Roger I'm doing okay I guess. You know, just the same ol' stuff I guess," Tara said putting her hand on my shoulder.

"Yeah I guess I do. Well I better get back to doing whatever I do here, want to have lunch today?" I asked as I usually do on Fridays. I know she'll say yes but I don't know why I bother with the formality of asking.

"Umm, yeah sure sounds great, is the usual spot okay? I got something I want your opinion on," she said.

I knew what that meant. That meant she's having problems with her boyfriend again. No big surprise there, the asshole doesn't realize what he has. He has the greatest woman I've ever met, and he treats her like shit.

"Sure thing Tara, See you around noon then?" I said and walk away. One day she'll realize how good of a guy I am. Someday she will love me.

I go back to my desk and change my desktop background to a picture of System of a Down I had taken at Ozzfest a few years back. The new mail icon flashed on the screen. Two new messages. First was from Human Resources, thanking me for applying but I wasn't selected for the consultant job I applied for two months ago. The second was a work assignment from Thomas. Nothing more insulting than that talentless sack of shit giving me orders.

I read his request and can't believe his stupidity. He can't figure out how to build a query for the database to only pull customers information from the last month, and he expects me to go through manually. I create the macro in minutes to do the task automatically and stare at the screen blankly. Random numbers scroll by like a stock ticker. It will probably take a half an hour for this to run its course, would have taken five hours to do this manually. One of these days this dumb company is going to realize the machines they pay us to operate could do our entire job for us, and do it more efficiently. It finishes in 34 minutes; I pretend to be working on it until lunch.

I lock my computer and head to the usual place, Subway. She's already waiting for me in our usual booth in the corner. She's never early; something really must be bothering her. "Do you want to talk now, or do you want to order first?" I ask.

"We better order, before it gets too busy," Tara said. We can usually beat the lunch crowd, but there's nothing worse than waiting for a mediocre sandwich.

"Okay," I said. I walk to the counter and give a nod to the worker the bread station. He asked me what I wanted sarcastically. I've come here twice a week for the last three years and my order hasn't changed once. Without even giving me the chance to answer he prepares my usual; 6-inch meat ball marinara on Italian herb bread, nothing on it except black olives and lettuce. Tara orders a vegetable sandwich with everything on it. I don't know why she thinks she needs to watch her weight, she's perfect. I get the combo with a drink and chips, which is always Funyuns. I think Funyuns are the most underrated of all chips. I pay for mine, and offer to pay for hers, she refuses. She always refuses.

We sit back down in our booth in the corner. I don't even fully unwrap my sandwich before she sits across from me. She pulls her long, straight brown hair into a ponytail. There's nothing she hates more than getting food in her hair, and never takes risks in regards to it. "So what is it you wanted to talk about, are you okay? You seem a little...off," I said taking a bite of my sandwich as an olive falls and sticks onto my shirt. I wait until she's not looking to pick it off and eat it.

"I know it's probably nothing, but he didn't call last night, and you know...my mind just wanders sometimes," Tara said as I start to see tears forming in the corner of her eyes. I put my hand on her soft shoulder. "Listen I'm sure he's fine, his mom would have called you if anything bad happened, you have your cell on you right?" She had a habit of losing important items, or leaving things at home when she needs them most. I always found it endearing, John, her boyfriend wasn't as amused by it.

"Yeah of course I do, I called him three times this morning with no answer," The tears well up in her eyes as she takes a bite of her sandwich as if to only keep the appearance that she's okay. "I don't think anything happened to him, I'm just afraid he's sleeping with his ex," she couldn't hold back the tears any longer. The more she fought them the more squeezed out. I slide my hand down onto her arm; this is the closest I'm ever going to get to holding her. This is as close as I'm ever going to get to embracing her the way I want to. "Look I'm sorry, and I'm sure that's not the case. I'm sure he's just sleeping in and there's nothing wrong. That makes the most logical sense right?"

"Yeah, I guess you're right. It does make the most sense, but you know with what he did before I can't help but think something is up."

"You know you deserve better Tara. You know you don't deserve to be treated like this right? You're one of the best people I've ever met. I'd give anything to have someone like you."

"I can't tell you what to do because I know it won't make a difference Tara, but I can always be here for you no matter what. Just know that okay?"

"Yeah, I know you will be, you always are and I

appreciate it."

"Let's just finish our lunch okay? If you want we can talk after work. How does that sound?

"Sounds good."

"Okay I'll meet you at your cube at 4:30 then?"

"Yeah."

We finish eating our lunch and walk back to work not saying a word to each other. I again greet the security guard with no response. There's a sticky note from Thomas left on my monitor telling me "good job on the report," like I need his thanks. He should be doing more than thanking me; I'm doing half of his damn job. The rest of the day passes quickly.

I arrive at her desk promptly at 4:30, Tara is on the phone. She turns around to me holding up one finger to let me know it'll just be a minute. I patiently wait and check my cell phone, no new messages, two new e-mails...both spam. I hear her hanging up the phone.

"You ready to go?" Tara said in a harsh tone.

"Yeah I guess so, are you okay?" She didn't respond she just walked towards the elevators. We wait for the elevator in silence. The door opens and we both step into the crowded elevator. My shoulder rubs up against hers due to the space constraint. If she only knew how much those little moments meant to me. She backs away and into someone else in the elevator. The elevator dings and the door opens for the first floor. We walk outside and she starts to speed up. "What's wrong? Did I do something?" Her only response is walking faster. I catch up. "Listen, I get it you're mad about something can you at least tell me?" My question was answered with more silence. She gets to her car in the garage and stops. No wait, she just can't find her keys. I grab her should and turn her around. "Talk to me damn it! Tell me what's going on," she's crying.

"I shouldn't talk to you anymore Roger, that's what's wrong," She's shaking.

"What are you talking about?" I ask.

"Don't pretend like you don't know why Roger," she said. Oh shit, she found out.

"You're a sex offender? How could you hide that from me? What kind of sick fuck are you?"

"It's not like that Tara, it wasn't anything bad, and it wasn't even my fault."

"If it's not your fault then why are you on the sex offender's website?"

"The bitch got mad that she lost her virginity to me, but I didn't want to marry her afterwords. She went to the police and said she was raped."

"You expect me to believe that? I thought we were friends Roger, fucking pervert. Never talk to me again. I never want to see you, you piece of shit."

"I..."

"Don't even try it mother fucker." How could she? Why won't she believe me? Why doesn't she see that I love her and care for her? That fucking bitch. I grab her by her long black hair, still in a ponytail.

"I love you Tara," I slam her head into the concrete column. "I fucking love you with everything I have Tara, and you do *this* to me? I slam her head into the cylinder again, and I hear a crack. Tara goes limp in my hands. I finally get to hold you. I go through her purse and find her keys. I grab her under her arms and drag her to the back seat and push her in. I throw her purse in the passenger seat and drive her car home.

When she awoke, she realized she was tied up to a wooden chair. She had never been in this part of my house before but the smell was unmistakable as a basement. Three inches in front of her face is a computer monitor. It's a display of a camera in the room. I could see her look into the monitor and realize she was looking at herself, but from a different angle. She looked up and saw the camera. I start my speech I wrote on a yellow legal pad.

"The problem with today's society is women. They've been given too much freedom and don't know what to do with it. A thousand years ago women were looking for a white knight, someone who could help her, someone that could protect her, someone that could provide for her. Not now.

Now all women are concerned with is how many tattoos he has, or what kind of motorcycle he drives off in after he beats your ass and apologizes. You'll keep letting him come back into your life even though deep down you know he'll never change. While I'm the guy you call when you are having problems with him. Just hoping you'd realize I was the one who loved you, the one that worshiped you. Who was the one who picked you up after he busted your lip? You laughed in my face when I told you I liked you and would do anything for you. Even after that I helped you study for your interview. You used me and you fucking know it! You knew how I felt about you, and you didn't care. You didn't care about my feelings, or the time I wasted on you.

It's despicable and you know it. Once I figured out I didn't have a shot or you didn't need me anymore how did you think I would react? You thought I would just cry about it and hopefully kill myself so you could pretend to care about me and get sympathy from all my real friends. Fuck you. You're not laughing right now are you? I'm going to kill him after this. I think if I get rid of him you will have to love me. Maybe some 'maniac' will run him off the road on his precious fucking motorcycle. The asshole deserves it for what he did to you, but you're too fucking dumb to realize I'm the one you need! ME! ME! ME! No matter how smart I am I couldn't capture your heart. All I wanted was for you to love me. You can't. You won't. I realize that now. There's nothing I can do. I am going to kill you. I'm going to do it streaming on the Internet so the whole fucking world can see what a worthless whore you are! Don't bother begging, it won't matter. Don't say you love me, we both know it's a lie. We could have been happy together," I said.

I open the basement door and carefully and slowly descended down the stairs. Making sure she heard every creak of every step. This is the only time she'd ever listen to me. The only time she'll be waiting in anticipation for me. I don't know why I almost liked her being afraid of me. I liked it more than the night she kissed me. Maybe because the kiss was a lie, this was real. I look her in the eyes and see the fear in them. She's still unsure if I'm going to go through with it. I check the computer to the side of the room, 128 viewers. The web cameras were all functioning perfectly. Three high definition camera's ready to spread my pain over the world.

"What do you have to say for yourself?" I ask.

"Please Roger, don't do this it's okay? I won't tell anyone" The panic in her voice is adorable.

"Shut your fucking whore mouth! You already heard what I said slut, and that's all you have to say? No 'it's not true it's not true it's not like that'? I do have to do this actually. Unless guys like me stand up to girls like you, it will never change. The whole world needs to see what happens when you fuck with a man's heart. You're going to be the zeitgeist of manipulative bitches."

"Yes I used you, yes it was a shitty thing to do Roger, but you have to realize that you let it happen, Roger! It's your fault you kept letting me do it. I knew you would never stand up to me; you would just keep doing whatever I asked. I did like you Roger, but you make it hard for me to respect you. You don't respect yourself enough to tell me to fuck off. I would have liked you more if you weren't a dickless, spineless asshole who can't accept that you can't have everything you want. If you wanted me to like you, you should have been someone I would have liked. Your mommy couldn't buy you love Roger," She said.

"Fuck you. Even if you're right, does it make it okay? Do you excuse Nazi's from shooting millions of Jews because they were given the opportunity? Maybe I was asking for it, but you still made the choice to do it to me. You can't justify doing that to someone. I'm still a fucking person Tara. I'm still a person with feelings, and emotions! There's no excuse for tearing my fucking heart out every day. This is the only way you'll learn from any of it. For you it's punishment, for me its revenge, for the world it's a learning experience," I said.

"I'm not going to change your mind, I know that, but can I just say a few last words to the world?" She said.

"I wish you would. Nothing would make me happier.

Let them all know how it feels to be who you are at a time like this."

"They can hear me right now?" She asked with tears dripping down her face.

"Yes."

"My name is Tara Redding, the sick fuck trying to kill me is Roger Pain that's P-A-I-N of Fort Worth Texas. 2703 Landry Rd someone call the police! This isn't a joke. He's going to kill me! Please help me!"I took the knife out of my pocket and sliced her across her cheek. I placed my hand across her throat and squeezed her windpipe. "Don't think that changes anything," I said. Blood starts trickling down from her cut in small streams. Every drop of blood won't equal every tear I shed for her, even if I drain her body out dry. It starts coming down her neck. I squeeze a little harder, her eyes widen. It makes me hard. No time to rape her as I had planned. The blood has started to run down her shirt, staining her collar. She knows what she did will make me have to hasten the process. I better get to work.

"I'm a whore all right? I'm a fucking whore," she confessed. "I can't fucking hear you!" I slice her other cheek.

"I'm a whore. Please, I'm just a whore. I'm a whore a whore a whore," her sobbing continues. "The world is seeing the whore I've seen in you for a long time." I make the next cut across her sternum, the letter "W" with sharp jagged points.

"What are you?"

"I'm a whore! Please don't," she says as I stab her with the scalpel and drag it down inch by inch. I cut into her again, doing the same about a half inch from the original wound. I cross the two lines as evenly as I can. "H".

"What are you?" I say, grinning.

"I'm a whore. I'm a whore, I'm a whore, I'm a whore, I'm a WHORE!"

"That's right, you are." I carve a near perfect circle directly below her throat, "O". Every incision makes me hate her just a little bit more. It's releasing all that anger I've felt for her in the last six years. "What are you?"

"I'm a whore." She is defeated. I carve the next letter, "R".

"What are you?"

"I'm a whore! I'm a dirty, filthy whore! The only reason I kissed you that night is because I just sucked him off. He thought it would be funny to kiss you after."

My eyes tear up. The only moment I felt loved was a practical joke. It stung, but no matter how many things she admits to, it won't change anything. I sink the entire blade into her skin and carve an "E".

"What does that spell?" The blood covers Tara like a coat, from clavicle to her slender legs. It slowly starts dripping onto the basement concrete.

"It makes me a whore and the world knows it. Now please, stop! You've made your point, just please stop," she says before I stop her.

"This is only a fraction of what you've done to me. This," I pause. "...is going to hurt."

I place my hand firmly against her neck, pressing the back of her head against the chair. Her skin is soft. I need to make sure she doesn't squirm. I make a six inch vertical incision below the "E" I just carved. She screams in pain, her feet kicking violently against the floor. "Don't pass out on me! You're not going to go into shock. Don't even fucking think about passing out!"

I make the second parallel incision. More screams, louder this time. I make the third and final cut connecting the first two. "See, that wasn't so bad, right?"

"Fuck you! You crazy son of a bitch, you dickless fucking nerd! There's a reason you don't have any friends! There's a reason even the sluts at work wouldn't fuck you!" I drop the scalpel. It makes several tinging noises on the solid concrete floor. I grab the flap of her skin and pull it down over her breast. The skin tears easily like ripping cardboard. The blood gushes out. She screams, and I squeeze her neck to muffle it. I can hear someone knocking at the door. My time is short. I have to act soon.

"That's how it felt the night I found out he hit you, and

you went back to him the next night!"

"Please! You're killing me!" Tara cries out. Her tears mix in with the blood on her face. I can see part of her ribcage.

"This is how it felt when I asked you out and your friends just laughed at me!" I grab the rib covering her heart. It's much slicker than I expect. I tug on the bone. I pull at the rib as if I was prying open an ancient tomb door. The sound of shards of bones splintering off as I pull at her rib drowns out her incessant sobbing. It snaps off in my hand. Dozens of fragments lodge into her now exposed heart. The screams are horrendous. As much as I want to hear them, they are almost too much. I can't imagine what it must feel like. What the fuck am I saying? This is what she did to me! She deserves this! I'm guessing the police just broke down my front door. It's only a matter of minutes before they find me down here. She vomits all over herself, her half digested sandwich spilling into her open wound.

"This is to show the world how much of a heartless bitch you truly are!" I plunge my right hand between her ribs and grab her erratically beating heart. I hear the police at the door of my basement shouting that they are coming in. There's no turning back now, I only have seconds to make this work.

A small task force busts through the door and tell me to drop my weapon. They want me to drop to the floor. The police notice where my hand is as they slowly close in on us. In a swift, single jerking motion, I pull the whore's heart out of her chest. She's looking at me. In her last seconds of life, she watches as I squeeze her heart now in my hands in front of her own eyes.

"This is what you did to me." Blood oozes out of it as I crush it with my bare hands, it deflates like a balloon. All the years of pain are gone. She's gone. Her lifeless, disfigured body stares back at me. She just like me now.

"I said don't fucking move, asshole!" one of the officers shouted.

"Why? What can you do to me now? The world already knows! The world has seen it all. Look!" I point to the cameras and monitors around the room. "The world knows what vile things she did to me."

"Last warning! Get on the floor NOW!" The second officer shouts with a gun pointed at my chest. I notice that he is in full swat gear. I take her heart, raise it to my mouth and bite into it. It was tougher to bite through than I thought, almost like a soft leather.

I spit out a chuck of her flesh and it lands on the plastic face mask of the officer closest to me. The chunk smears blood across the glass as gravity forces it to the ground with a single wet plop. "How many people must I kill for her to love me?" I ask. My left leg explodes in pain as the police office shoots me in my knee. Two other officers jump on top of me and struggle to hold me down. My head hits the cold concrete and creates a gash just above my eyebrow.

I turn my head to the side and say, "It doesn't matter what you do to me...the world already knows."

The Body of Roger Pain

The Geek's head jerked back as a geyser of blood exploded from the hole in his head. The Cannibal wasted little time. The gun dropped from his hand and onto the floor as he attacked The Geek's neck, biting into his jugular vein. Relief washed over him as The Geek's blood soaked The Cannibal. He ran his tongue across his front teeth to taste his cure. Like a fine wine, The Cannibal wanted to savor this moment.

The Cannibal took a finger and placed it deep inside the wound in The Geek's head. He could feel the slick covering of the brain. The Cannibal took his finger out and savored the taste of The Geek, his rich meat as good as cake batter. The guards walked into the execution room. They knew the rumors about The Cannibal's blood lust, but they were still surprised of how heavily The Cannibal fought to keep from removing The Geek's body.

His finger was still deep inside the skull when he kicked one of the guards in the shin. Seconds later, the guard slammed his face hard into the table. The harder he resisted the more strength it took to keep the Cannibal's face pressed down against the cold surface of the table. The Short Guard was afraid that The Cannibal's skull would crack if he didn't stop resisting. The Tall Guard dragged The Geek's body away, leaving a trail of blood and skull fragments. Everyone in the room was silent except The Cannibal who was muttering to himself. The Woman was disgusted by the atrocity that had just occurred ~~moments before~~ right next to her.

The Gangster ~~was~~ silently assessing his fellow inmates, looking for any sign of weakness that they may have. He didn't mind dying, but he didn't want his mother to see him lying in a casket with half of his face gnawed off. The Pacifist sat perplexed, trying to analyze what he had just witnessed. The only cannibal he had heard of was Hannibal Lector, a brilliant fictional man who loved the taste of flesh. What he had just witnessed was a cross between absolute madness and barbarism. He could only figure that there was no sanity left in this man, only primal instincts.

The Cannibal cried. He clenched his hands into fists and slammed them hard onto the table with an alarming thud. Blood splattered around the table as he did so. He noticed a small amount of brain matter at his feet. Scooping up the slimy grey matter up, he closed his eyes and smiled. He relished the taste as he placed it into his mouth. He was happy, relaxed, and content for the moment. The Short Guard took the remaining two bullets out of the gun's chamber. "Eight more to go fellas." At this point, though, the other inmates seemed like the secondary threat compared to The Cannibal. The Short Guard placed a new bullet into the chamber and handed it to the only woman within the room.

The Woman

The Woman was covered with The Geek's blood as it spurted from the wound. She wiped away a chunk of skull fragment from her cheek, not aware the blood that covered her face at all. For the last 10 minutes, she was in shock. The reality of the atrocity that had just occurred finally hit The Woman.

She was convicted of two murders. They were gruesome, but were nothing like this. She murdered out of her hatred for men, but this was different. This was a mix of insanity and instincts. The Cannibal wasn't even human in her eyes, he was a beast in human skin. There was no reasoning with him. She also felt no remorse for putting him down like the beast he was.

She knew no one would blame her if she killed him. Everyone was in agreement that The Cannibal would need to be killed next. They may be strangers, but they all knew they didn't want to be eaten, or see anyone be eaten again. "Who would want to keep this unpredictability around?" The woman thought. Her paranoia began to kick in.

"It's only a matter of time before these guys start talking and forming alliances like some sort of stupid reality TV show," she thought to herself. No one would want to keep The Cannibal. The tattooed asshole wouldn't even be that crazy. No one will want revenge on The Woman if she killed him.

"Hey, you sick son of a bitch! You only have a few minutes left. I hope you're ready to die," The Woman said, bringing everyone's attention on her instead of The Cannibal.

"You don't understand! It didn't work!" The Cannibal sobbed. His body was covered with dried blood and gore.

"No, I understand! I understand that I'm going to blow your fuc..."

The Cannibal interrupted her. "The Dragons, They lied to me again! They lied to me *again*! Why am I so stupid?" He whimpered.

"I'm going to lodge this bullet in between your eyes, you fucking disgusting sack of shit!" The Woman said grinning slightly.

"Hey, do what you want. But maybe you shouldn't piss off the guy whose eating people," The Terrorist said from the other side of the table.

"I don't want to die! I just want to be cured!" The Cannibal was sobbing hysterically.

"Listen, I think we can all agree on this. We have enough shots to make sure this asshole doesn't get the chance at another one of us again. Can we agree to just end this miserable faggot's life?" The Woman said, trying to form some kind of order to their deaths.

"Maybe we want to see you eaten, baby girl," The Gangster replied.

"I've had men with better tongues than yours feasting on me, honey," The Woman shot back. For her, being a stripper paid well enough, but everyone knew the real money wasn't on *the* pole, it was on *his* pole. "We all know black guys don't go down on their chicks," The Woman said.

"Can you blame us? No man should kneel down to a ~~woman.~~ bitch Besides, the nasty bitches like you always got nasty pussies," The Gangster replied.

"How do you know if you never try, hotshot?" The Woman shot back.

"I ain't trying to be rude or nuthin', but you don't have to take the pants off of some of these bitches before the steamin' clam chowder hits you in your face," The Gangster said grinning. He liked referring to a vagina as a clam. His grandmother had taught him that, telling him that he would never find a pearl in the clam bed.

"Look, I don't think this is a difficult situation in our hands here. We're pretty much all going to end up dead in the next hour or so, but I think we can all say without a doubt we don't want that crazy people-eating-asshole being the one that walks out of here alive," The Woman said. She stood with her hands planted palm down like she was a general discussing attack plans over a war room table.

"I'm not a fucking animal, I have a disease!" The Cannibal cried. "I just need the cure to get back to normal."

"The only cure for you is when one of us puts a bullet in your fucking brain," The Gangster said. He made a gun with his hand and winked as he pulled down his thumb with a pop.

The buzzer went off. She grabbed the pistol in one hand and pointed it to the man immediately to her right. The Cannibal was sobbing again. She, nor anyone else in the room, felt any remorse for him. There was no hesitation as she cocked back the hammer and pulled the trigger.

-Click-

The Preacher

Like an assembly line procedure, The Woman handed the gun to the next person. Everyone knew what to expect at this point. The gun was in the hands of The Preacher, the obese black man in the room. He had been completely silent since the horrible death of The Geek. He hadn't been listening to the squabble between The Woman and The Gangster. It didn't matter to him. The Preacher knew he didn't have what it took to win. His life was over. His everyday boring life as a preacher had been over for three years now. He resigned himself to the fact that he would die in this room. He had never suffered from depression, but he knew this game was hopeless. He only wanted to see his family one last time, but he also knew that wasn't going to happen. He placed another bullet in the chamber.

"Hey everyone, I know we're in this fucked up situation, and there's nothing we can do about it. I don't want my last potential minutes to be unpleasant. Please, everyone tell a little something about yourself so we don't all die strangers," The Preacher said. He pointed at the man covered with the various tattoos and facial piercings. "You go first."

The Hitman sat in quiet contemplation for a moment, taken back by the question. He had never been asked before to introduce himself. "Hello. I, uh, guess it doesn't really matter what I say, does it? I guess instead of telling you about myself, I'll tell you what I believe. That's what really matters, right? It's not what you've been through, but what those experiences make you think and feel, right?" The Hitman pondered. "I believe we're all fucked because of what we've done. Nothing is going to change that. All we can do is learn from it before we catch a bullet in the face."

"All we should be doin' is prayin' to the Lord for forgiveness." For the first time, The Gangster was being serious.

"Fuck your Lord," The Hitman said. "I never understood that entire thing, how white guys will always find religion after committing a crime, but black guys will find it *while* doing a crime."

"It's all we got back in the ghetto, man. You gotta find hope somewhere out there, it sure as hell ain't in the streets," answered The Gangster. He was irritated but it hadn't offended him. He always found that piece of black culture strange as well.

"I guess I don't have anything else to say. I know I won't get out of here anyways. We aren't exactly expected to buddy up over the next few hours," The Hitman sighed.

"Okay, you're next," The Preacher pointed at The Gangster.

"Um, well, I guess the easiest way to tell the story of my life is to just say 'I got caught up'. I grew up in Fort Worth with my mom and my four brothers. Mom got sick and couldn't work when I was 14, so me and my brothers hit the streets. We did what we had to do to get by. We told her we had jobs with 'computers'. Funny how you can just say 'computers' like it means something, but she believed us anyways. Or at least we believed that she believed us. I met a girl, had a baby, and life was all good. Then a robbery went bad, shit turned bad real quick, and I ended up here. End of story," The Gangster said. "I guess you're up, joker." The Gangster pointed to the snarky man next to him.

"Hey, look at that, it's me. I'll keep this brief because you probably already know a bit about me," The Serial Killer said. "I'm the Prairie Dog Killer. I'm the guy who used to pick up whores from clubs, bars, and even homeless shelters and give them a new home...in the lake!" He laughed. "I hate that name though! Out of all the lakes I could have dumped those whores in, it had to be the Prairie Dog Lake. I didn't even know it had a name! Thirteen whores in all, though the prosecutor tried to pin me for every raccoon that washed up on those banks for the last twenty years." The Woman bit her lip, trying to hold back the anger that was showing on her face.

"That wasn't exactly what I had planned, but I guess I should have expected it," The Preacher said. "My name is Stanley Williams. I grew up in Chicago. I moved out here for a job, a chance for my own church. I was accused of touching the boys in the choir by the elders who didn't like me, and the plans I had for the church. The rumor spread to the point where police got involved. How could people who claimed to be followers of Christ do something as evil as accuse their spiritual leader of something so evil? It made me lose my faith not only in God, but in humans as well. "I couldn't allow such evil people to live in this world any longer. What good is a preacher who has lost his faith? It's like a pianist without fingers. I've wandered lost ever since. I wanted to kill myself but I couldn't do it. Even though that's all I wanted to do. It was supposed to be my last righteous act. "This time I feel like The Lord is on my side," The Preacher cried. "Please forgive me Kimberly." He placed the cold barrel of the gun in his mouth, clenched down on it with his teeth, and pulled back the trigger.

Russian Poker

R.L. Murphy

-Bang-

The Story of Stanley Waters

"How many do I have to kill for them to believe me?"

I wake up to a thud on my front door. Several teenagers are yelling outside my house. I hear the car pulling away before I can make it to the window. I run outside. I don't care that I'm just in my boxers. The punks sprayed "Burn In Hell PERVERT" on my front door with red spray paint. No reason to take it off, they'll just spray it back on within a week. I go back inside and open the refrigerator door.

I grab the orange juice and drink straight from the carton. Since Ashley left me, there's no reason not to drink out of the carton. I step back into my bedroom.

I really don't feel like taking a shower today. I put on the first pair of jeans I see on the floor, and pull a random button-up shirt from my closet. The worst part about being as fat as I am is there are no acceptable fat stores in this town. Any self-respecting woman can walk into a Lane Bryant and not feel like they are in a fat store, but anytime you walk into a men's "Big and Tall" store, you immediately feel like you should be in a zoo. Maybe I already am in a zoo. I pull two socks out of my top dresser drawer.

I never care if they match as long as they feel good on

my feet. I find my shoes in their regular spot and put them on. As I walk to my car, I see two female joggers passing by my home. They are both white and attractive, and both are staring daggers at me. I hang my head, avoiding their stare, and grab my keys out of my pocket.

I get inside my car, the leather interior already hot enough to burn skin. I knew I shouldn't have bought this car with its leather interior, it retains too much heat in the summer, and it always feels like summer in Texas. I need to stop at the store to purchase snacks for the children. I might as well get something for myself. Today is my last sermon. I pull into the parking space near the entrance of Tom's Groceries.

I always love that first couple of steps inside, that first rush of cold air as it wraps your body all over. Nothing beats the feeling of air conditioning hitting you in the face with the scent of a fresh bakery and produce. Should I get a cart or just a basket? I think a basket is fine, but who really ever uses these things?

Health food nuts say you should only shop on the outside of the store and anything in the aisles is bad for you. I like to try to follow their advice so I head to the bakery and straight for fresh donuts. I guess I should know better than to feed the children donuts and juice, but it is up to their parents if they allow them to have the donuts. It's okay though, I haven't had my breakfast yet. I'll take a couple out for myself.

I accidentally bump into someone as I walk to the checkout lanes. "Excuse me, I'm sorry," I apologize.

"Is that how you introduce yourself to little boys too? By 'accidentally' bumping into them? I bet that got your dick hard, didn't it, faggot? Go kill yourself! You deserve it, you fat fuck!" He said as he aggressively pokes me in my chest with a finger. When I looked up, I see that this man appears to be in his mid-thirties, and I suspect that he probably spends his Saturday nights watching NASCAR.

"I didn't do it! How many people do I have to convince of this? How many polygraph tests do I need to take for you to believe me? How many prayers do I have to say before anyone but God believes me?" I say.

"Lemme tell you something, you piece of shit! God doesn't believe someone who did what you did. Everyone knows, so just admit it." I walk away tired of explaining myself. It's not even 9 A.M. yet. The man yells across the store "You're going to burn in hell motherfucker! When you go to prison, you're going to get what's comin' to ya! They gonna make you feel the pain you caused them, you prick!" I know I didn't do anything, and God knows too, so what else matters? I rush to the nearest empty checkout line I see. I just want to hurry up and leave.

"Good morning, how are you doing today?" I try my best to be pleasant with the cashier. She doesn't reply until all of my items are scanned and bagged.

"That will be four dollars and eighty eight cents. Cash or credit?"

"Cash," I respond. I open my leather wallet and remove a five dollar bill. It's the last bit of tender in my wallet. She takes it without saying a word.

She grabs my change and says, "Twelve cents is your change. Have a good day."

"You too, hun. Take it easy and God bless."

"Don't call me 'hun', sir. I turned 18 last week. I'm too old for you," she says nonchalantly. I try to ignore the comment, and I hurry out of the store and towards my car. I unlock my car door and shove the grocery bag in the passenger seat. I turn up the radio on my way to church. I always loved sports radio even though I never really liked sports. It's just nice to hear people talk about things they are passionate about besides hating me. Around these parts, third string quarterbacks from a decade ago can get a radio show people will listen to religiously. They keep talking about statistics I don't know anything about. Something about the 1972 Dolphins not being as good statistically as the 1985 Bears, whatever that means.

The radio goes into a commercial about the local sporting goods store. I used to go there with my dad for fishing supplies. This country has lost the American value of fathers explaining life to their boys on a lake. I think the children would be a lot better off if more fathers took their sons fishing, even if the fish wouldn't.

The sports program starts again as I turn into the church parking lot, North East Baptist Church. I gave my life to the Lord and to this church, but what good is it if no one comes? It's just a building if no one is in it. It's the people that make the church, not the wood and windows. The people inside this church are termites, slowly eating away at the foundation that let them live fruitfully. I grab the juice and donuts and make my way inside. I always loved the smell of this place. So clean, so holy, so...sacred. I make my way to the little kitchenette we called the water cooler room, and brew a pot of coffee.

I walk outside to the expansion we had built for the children of my congregation. It's nice that they have a friendlier environment to worship in. It's always struck me as peculiar how in Sunday school the children are taught about God's love for you and how He has great things planned for your life, but when as an adult you learn if you disobey God, He will do terrible things to you. I always strive to give a happier, more inspirational message that continues the gospel of love and forgiveness. I unlock the doors of the Sunday school and flick the light switch. Paper drawings of crayon Jesus and marker bible stories decorate the walls of the Sunday school.

I wait for Kimberly to arrive in the Sunday school

extension. She will have today's lesson all planned out, she's always prepared. I go back into the church and check on the coffee. The fresh aroma that permeates the air lets me know that it's done. I grab a mug with the church's name on it out of the cabinet above the coffee pot and pour myself a cup. I never like to drink any more than a half cup at a time, I get too jittery. I head into the back of the church where my office is to make sure the supplies are ready. I just need to wait for the right time, and hope God lets everything else go as planned. As I head back outside towards the Sunday school, I see a white Honda Accord park next to my car. A woman in her mid-twenties steps out of the car. I say to her, "Good morning Kimberly. How are you doing on this fine day?"

"I'm doing well, Stanley. Is the coffee ready?" She asks.

"Of course, you know me, coffee lets God's words flow through my body." She smiles a smile that could brighten anyone's day.

"I know it's unlike me, but I had a long night and need a bit of a pick me up," Kimberly said. I wasn't too old to realize what having a long night meant.

"You know I drink it black, but I think there might be a few packets of sugar in the drawer below the pot."

"Okay, thanks Stanley."

"Hey, I just wanted to tell you, you were always great to me, and you've been a great help through everything that's been going on around here. I guess what I'm trying to say is, I really appreciate everything you do."

"Aw, thanks Stanley. You've given me light at my darkest hours, so the appreciation goes both ways." She slips her arms around me and I hug her back. Kimberly steps inside the church for coffee, leaving me behind to stand on the steps to greet people as they show up. As cars begin to fill the parking lot, I try to greet my congregation with a handshake. Many people refused, some just give me a look as if I was Pontius Pilate and I was personally responsible for nailing Jesus to the cross.

When the majority of the congregation has entered, I step inside the church for the last time. I see the elders of the church whispering amongst each other, spreading their hatred. They look up and see me. I can sense them spewing their malicious rumors for the last time. They know what they've done, and they know they are wrong, but they enjoy this. The rest of the flock is mingling as usual. I overhear Mrs. Waters speaking about which church her family is going to attend after I resign. I hear Mr. Hinton talking about how he doesn't believe in the rumors, but it's still unsettling. I see the children playing in the aisles, running around and laughing, not paying any attention to what their parents are discussing.

"I couldn't find the cream or sugar so I just drank it black," Kim says and smiles at me. I've always had a little crush on Kimberly, but I knew that she wouldn't want anything to do with me. The way she smiles, though, makes my heart quiver.

"No matter what happens, take care of the kids, okay? I mean, always do what's best for them, okay? No matter what happens with all of this. Can you do that for me?"

"Yes, I suppose so. Just know I love those kids, and it pains me that I can't be near them during this big ordeal. Just make sure they are taken care of, okay?"

"Okay, I'll be ready as soon as this coffee kicks, which will hopefully be soon." I watch her as she walks outside, leaving her Styrofoam cup of coffee on the counter with a lipstick stain on the rim. I make my way down the aisle and step up to the pulpit. I clear my throat and begin to speak into the microphone. "Just want to make sure the PA system is working. We will be starting here in just a few minutes. I have a special announcement planned for today." I go back to my office just behind the altar and sneak the supplies for today's sermon behind the curtain. I carefully emerge from behind the curtain to see the last of the flock walking through the open door. I stand at the pulpit waiting for everyone to settle down.

"As a minister, I've grown to love all of you. However, with the exception of God, just because you love something, doesn't mean it'll love you back. I've learned this recently. I've done nothing but pour my heart and soul into this building, to give others the joy that God has given me. I never enjoyed preaching about punishment that God will lay upon you if you disobey Him because I believed we were not the ones disobeying. Or, at least, that's what I thought." I close my eyes and take a deep breath.

"I've been quiet about everything. I haven't bothered to say anything about what's going on for good reason. I didn't want to do anything to bring attention to these slanderous rumors and only make it worse. However, I can't do that anymore. This has gone too far. A great evil has been done here, and I believe most of you are not to blame. The elders of this church, who have been going to this church before I even began preaching here, are corrupt. They will do anything or say anything they have to, to get their way. They don't care how evil the consequences are. This experience has ruined my career, my whole life, and there's nothing you can say or do to make this better. I know you are expecting me to resign, to just give up, but that's not what I have ever done in life, and I'm not going to start now." I step behind the curtains and find the gas cans I left behind there. I unscrew the lids and carry them out.

"Yes. Fortunately the Sunday school teacher reacted quickly and got all the kids out of there safely, but I'm sorry to say she's not doing too well." Laying on the grass, I turn my head to the side. I force my eyes fully open. Kimberly is laying beside me, smiling at me. "I had to make sure the kids were safe, right boss? I hope I did okay."

"The coffee, I forgot my cup of coffee." She is struggling for air, but continues. "I forgot my coffee. I went back for it but the doors were locked. I smelt the smoke so I called for help. I'm sorry, Stanley. I'm sorry I couldn't do more." Her eyes close. I roll over and place my hand on her cheek. God bless you, Kimberly. I pass out again.

The Body of Stanley Waters

Stanley Water's enormous body slumped over the cold metal table with a resounding thud a second after the bullet pierced his skull. The lasting vibrations shook the inmates all the way down to The Pacifist on the other side of the table. The Hitman noticed tendrils of smoke escaping from of the gaping hole tracked by the bullet. Blood crawled across the table as Stanley stared blankly back at The Hitman sitting beside him.

The prison guards watched the violence through the two-way mirror that separated them from the chaos. The guards let the body lay there in the room with the inmates for a few moments. They could have come in as soon as they heard the shot, but instead they reveled in making the prisoners wait. They wanted them to think that maybe they wouldn't come back this time.

The guards casually walked inside the room, not concerned with the violence that had just occurred. The Tall Guard tried his best to pry the weapon from of the grip of Stanley Waters without success. The Short Guard stepped in, cracking the bones of Stanley's fingers, one by one, until the grip was loosened and the gun fell freely into The Short Guard's hands. He handed the gun back to The Tall Guard as he watched over the prisoners to make sure none of them tried to escape. They knew that it would take at least two guards to move Stanley's girth out of this room. They hollered for another guard for assistance. The Short Guard hugged Stanley around the waist while the third guard grabbed the body by the feet. The Tall Guard removed the bullet from the chamber and replaced it with a fresh one. He laid the weapon down in front of the next inmate in line to shoot, The Hitman.

The Hitman

The Hitman smiled as he picked up the gun. He thought he knew what type of weapon he was holding from observing it when The Preacher used it. He was certain It was a Smith & Wesson Model 686, he was right. He was well acquainted with this type of gun. It was the first pistol he had ever owned. He liked the fact it could hold not only the .357 magnum bullets, but would also fire the bullets from a .38 Special. He never used the same bullet type for consecutive jobs to throw off cops. The grip on this particular pistol was different than his old standby. He had his modified with a wood grip, and this was the standard rubber. The Hitman wondered if this pistol was merely a coincidence, or if the guards were giving him a slight advantage in this game.

"Look, what The Preacher did should have been expected. We all knew that one of us would crack under this pressure," The Hitman said.

"Stanley," The Woman cried out. "His name was Stanley. At least have the respect to call him by his name," she said as she glanced over at the vacant seat beside her.

"So when you first saw him, you didn't think to yourself 'Wow, that guy's a big fat fuck?'" mocked The Hitman.

"That doesn't mean he's not still a person with his own thoughts and feelings," The Woman replied.

"The bullet he blasted into his own skull makes him not a person," The Hitman joked. "We can't change what happened to him. There's only one guy in this room we all can agree we want dead, and that's you, nutcase," The Hitman said and aimed the gun at The Cannibal's forehead. The room fell silent.

"You don't understa..," The Cannibal wailed and was interrupted.

"We understand that we don't want you munching on anyone else. I'm sure if there's a news story about this whole thing, you eating us will be the highlight, and not who makes it out of here alive. I suggest we don't shoot one another until the fucktards spying on us drag his body out. So let's get back to our awkward silence and let the Dahmer party over there contemplate his last hour," The Hitman snickered again, exposing his near toothless grin.

The Cannibal cried, muttering to himself in between sobs. He wasn't getting any sympathy from the other prisoners. They knew what had to be done. Even The Gangster, who still wanted revenge over the racial slur from The Innocent, was willing to put his differences aside to ensure that his mother didn't have to read the reports of her son being murdered then feasted upon.

Six shots would take place before The Cannibal received the gun again. No one wanted to be the one to miss the shot.

Missing the shot or if one of the inmates strayed from the plan meant that the bullet count got reset, and the Cannibal would have his chance again. Looking at one another, they all made a silent pact about what had to be done. No one said a word.

The buzzer sounded. The Woman jumped in her seat. The ringing surprised her every time.

"Alright cocksucker, here's your fucking medicine," The Hitman shouted.

"Please don't! I don't want this! I just want to be cured! The Dragons, they promised me! They lied to me," The Cannibal pleaded.

"Don't bother, fuck-face! I won't make you wait. You don't deserve the extra few seconds of life." The Cannibal stared directly down the barrel of the gun. The Hitman's arm was steady and his aim, precise. He knew if the gun went off, this would be over. "Rest in peace, nut job." The Hitman pulled the trigger.

-Click-

The Gangster

The Cannibal was elated when he realized he wasn't dead yet. He clapped his hands together with delight. "Don't celebrate for too long. You're still as good as gone in everyone's eyes," The Gangster said. He searched through the mound of bullets on the metal table, looking for just the right bullet to lodge into The Cannibal's face.

"What the fuck are you doing there, OG?" said The Serial Killer.

"I gotta find the right bullet. You know, the one that's gonna go rip that motherfucker's head clean off his shoulders." The Gangster nodded towards The Cannibal.

"Hold up! You believe it matters what bullet you pick and that this is not just blind fucking luck? If luck had anything to do with it, we wouldn't be here! In case you didn't notice, we all got caught," The Serial Killer said.

"My momma always told me to be a little superstitious, just in case. What could it hurt?"

"It hurts your integrity, pal! It's bullshit and we all know it, even you," said the Serial Killer.

"Maybe to you, but if it even has the slightest advantage of getting rid of that fucking nutcase out of here a few minutes quicker, why not give it a shot? We gotta blow this ten minutes anyways." The Gangster chose a bullet near the center of the pile of bullets, placed it between his thumb and index finger, an held it up to the light. "Gotta good feeling about this one. Yeah, I think this will do just fine. This piece of steel is gonna be the one that'll blow your fucking brains out."

"I don't think I can be killed. The Dragons told me. The Dragons are letting me live until I find the cure. It won't matter what bullet you pick. The Dragons...They told me you picked the wrong one. They want me to find my cure," said The Cannibal.

The Gangster looked at The Cannibal calmly. "See this little piece of metal here in my hand? This is the piece of metal that's going to be lodged in your skull here in just a few minutes," He said loading the bullet into the chamber of the gun. He spun the chamber and listened calmly to the clicks, clicks, clicks, spinning before slamming it back into place. He placed the gun on the table, confident his shot was a sure thing. He placed his hands behind his head, and locking his fingers in place and leaned back in his chair. "Well, I think we owe it to the recently departed to finish up introducing ourselves. Half of you fuckers haven't said a peep, especially you, Arab."

"Do you even know what Arab means? Ignorant American, piece of shit," the Terrorist said. "My family is from Iran, but I was born in Columbus, Ohio. I'm more American than the Governor of California. I'm the first person to be sentenced to the death penalty for espionage in this country since World War Two. I'm just going to assume you dropped out of high school before learning what that means. So I'll spell it out for you: I was charged with being a spy."

"Big shocker there! I know a terrorist when I see one," said The Innocent. The buzzer went off. The Terrorist stared The Innocent down. Not being one to give a shit about the petty squabble going on, The Gangster picked the gun up from the table, and aimed his fateful shot at The Cannibal's skull. The Terrorist made a gun hand at The Innocent. The Terrorist winked at The Innocent as if he was aiming down the cross hairs of a rifle. The Cannibal just smiled.

"You picked the wrong bullet! You picked the wrong bullet! That one will never go off! It won't kill me! No bullet will ever kill me," The Cannibal laughed. The Gangster extended his arm, aimed, and pulled the trigger.

"Night night mother fucker!"

-Click-

The Serial Killer

The Cannibal was still smiling. "See, I told you! You picked the wrong one! Ha ha! I saw the right one. The Dragons told me. You were so close," The Cannibal said.

"Shut the fuck up!" The Gangster said.

"What? You mean, you know the secret of the curse of the Dragons?" The Cannibal's heart sank.

"What? What the fuck are you talking about? No! It means we're going to splatter your brains on that wall right behind you. And just because it wasn't me, doesn't mean it won't be any of these four motherfuckers....wait, oh shit!" The Gangster had an epiphany. By the time the gun would get to The Pacifist, it would have all six bullets in the chamber. He also knew that The Pacifist refused to shoot anyone, and had urged the others to do the same. The Gangster knew he didn't have the highest IQ in this room, but he knew he was right about this. They all look at The Pacifist.

"I will not shoot him. I don't care how many people he chooses to eat in front of us, it's not right to kill him," The Pacifist professed.

"What's not right is we may end up giving you a guaranteed kill and you're going to shoot the tiles?" The

Gangster asked.

"That is correct."

"That's fucked!"

"What kind of world are we in when *not* murdering is considered 'fucked' as you put it?"

The Serial Killer interrupted. "Look, do the math. It won't get that far. We're just speculating what could happen. I will have a fifty-fifty shot, then it's going to pass to Abdul over there, and he's going to get two thirds shot. Then after that, it's goes to Mr. Racial Slur over there with only one empty chamber. It ain't even worth talkin' about. Pac-Man over there is going to get his in no time."

The Gangster handed The Serial Killer the gun. The Serial Killer mockingly started digging through the bullets. "Oh, I gotta find the bullet that my momma would want me to kill a cannibal with, right? I'm not superstitious, but if I don't act like it, my other black friends will think I'm weird!" The Gangster was offended by his impression.

"Laugh it up, Prairie Dog. Was muskrat ravine already filled up with hookers?" The Gangster said. The Woman put a hand to her face, doing her best to hold back her laughter.

"Now, you know I *hate* that shit! Why do you gotta do that? I'm not even in a place where I can shoot you in good conscience."

"Just havin' a little fun. I thought you'd appreciate

having some laughs at your own expense," The Gangster said.

The Buzzer went off. The Serial Killer picked up the gun, and took a few seconds to aim. The Cannibal stood still, sure that The Dragons hadn't lied to him.

"Yeah, right there. Hey, tampon licker! Do you have any last words before I pull this trigger? Anything you want to say that we can remember you by?"

"I just wa.."

-Bang-

The Story of Willy Beacon

"How many must I kill before I'm cured?

Tonight's the night. The full moon is out. They told me it only works on the full moon. They've lied to me before. I don't think they are lying this time. They know the cure. They know I need it. They know I'll do anything for it. They know I'll vanish soon. I'm no good to them invisible. The Dragons know.

My house smells like cat piss again. I hate cat piss. Tonight is the night. I put on my purple sweat pants. The ones mom bought for me. It was the last thing she gave me. The roaches on the wall are funny. I love them. Where do they think they are going? Why are they in such a hurry? What are they hiding from? Is it me? I'm going to vanish soon. Unless I get the cure. The roaches want to disappear. I want to stay seen. They should ask The Dragons for my curse. Then they will vanish forever.

I need breakfast even though it's almost night. My kitchen is good. I look at my cereal boxes on the counter. They make me laugh. They never say the word "sugar" anymore. Like it's a bad word. It's a wonderful word. Mom killed herself and I scrubbed the blood out of the carpet. Back then, cereals said "sugar" on the box. Sugar Flakes, Sugar Wheels, Sugar

Smacks, Sugar Cones. They all had the word "sugar" on them. Now Mom is gone. So is the sugar on the box.

There's no clean bowls. The blue one in the sink is mostly clean. I'll use that one. Only a few dried flakes stuck to the side. I open the refrigerator door. No milk. Filtered water, mustard, orange juice, mayonnaise, ketchup, soy sauce, and relish. I'll use orange juice. There's sugar in orange juice. I pour the cereal into the bowl. I shake the orange juice. I pour it over the cereal. I like the pulp the best. I find my clean spoon and eat my breakfast. Twelve essential vitamins. I can only taste ten. I can't even name twelve vitamins. The orange juice makes the cereal taste bitter. I eat it anyways. One last flake on the side of the bowl. I better eat it.

"You know what you have to do tonight?" A voice says.

"Oh no, why you? Why today?" I say back to the voice.

"You know why. You need the cure to break the curse that we placed on you."

"Stupid Dragons. Stupid scales. I don't want the cure, just leave me alone!" I see him, I see the Dragons! They are right in front of me. Just inches away from me. I can feel their fire, so hot, in their throats.

"If you find the cure and stop the disease, you won't disappear anymore. I can bring your mother back. But you know

the deal. Unless, of course, you don't want to see her again,"
The Dragons laughed at me. The big flames came out of their
nostrils.

"No, no please! I need the cure, I need it! Please
don't leave! I need it! I'll do anything, anything for the cure! I
need my mother back," I pleaded to The Dragons. "I miss her. I
need her. I don't want to clean her from the carpet again. I
want to hug her. I want her to push me on the swings again.
Mommy, I need you."

"Okay Dragons, I'll do it. Just tell me what I need to
do." The Dragons could tell I was going to cry.

"Stop your crying! You must never, ever allow your
emotions to take control. If you do, you're going to lead
yourself into a really nasty predicament."

"Okay Dragons."

"I need you to do what you failed to do last time. Do
you know what I'm talking about?"

"I think so."

"You didn't follow through on your previous
attempts. I don't want persistent failure."

"I didn't know the rules! How was I supposed to
know?"

"Use your head or I'll annihilate you."

"Yes Dragon...sir." I look down at my feet. I need to
clip my toe nails. No time. "How do you want me to do it?" I

get no response. I look up. The Dragons are gone. I don't like them anyways. I just need the cure. I'm not a failure! They just won't give it to me!

I look around on the floor in my room. Socks, socks, socks, where are my socks? I see two. They are in front of the couch. One of them looks okay. It's only got brown spots on the toes. The other one is crusty. Is that the one I've been beating off on? It don't matter. A sock is just a sock. It smells like sour milk. It's not important.

I see my shoes. They are poking out from under my bed. I always take them off at my bed. Right before I sleep. So the roaches won't have more of a chance to get in them. These are the best shoes I've ever had. Mom took me to get new shoes one time. She told me that these shoes give you a new balance. I guess that's why they are called New Balance. I don't trip anymore. I guess it worked ever since.

Shit, I almost forgot my supplies! On the first time, The Dragons told me I had to bring three tools with me on every quest. I always keep them in my backpack. I unzip it to make sure they are still there. The knife with a five inch blade...check. Unscented hand sanitizer...check. Black leather gloves...check. I've love smelling them when I take them out of the bag. I wear the backpack with just one strap, like the cool kids who beat me up in high school. Maybe I can be cool now. For now I just walk and walk and walk until The Dragons tell me where the cure is.

Who has the cure? I don't want to die, especially because of a curse. They made me have it.

Sarah Lane, take a left. I love Sarah Lane. The houses all have flowers. All the houses look the same, but they all have different flowers around them. Thirty one sixty mostly has sunflowers. That's my favorite flower. They have a garage but there's a Toyota Yaris in the driveway. I like that car, it makes me think of turtles with wheels. This must be a sign, this must be the house. I can feel it. Why does grass get wet at night? It's not raining and the grass is always wet.

I keep walking by all the houses and they still look the same, especially in the dark. I bet whoever made these houses made a shit load of cash on them. I don't want a shit load of cash, I just want the cure.

I circle around the house. I need a safe place to get into the house. It's dark enough out that they won't see me. My New Balance will make sure I don't make noise. Kitchen windows are latched, and the back door is locked. No alarm system, it would have gone off when I tried to open the door. Unless it's a silent alarm, but I don't hear anyone in the house either. There is no way in unless I make a lot of noise. Wait, I got it!

I open up my backpack. I take out the leather gloves. I put on the left, pulling it down with my teeth. Then I use my left hand and put the right glove on. I use my teeth again. I love the taste of leather. I killed a cow once and tried to eat it, but it didn't taste like leather. Why not? I close my eyes and smell them both. I get the knife out of the bag. The electrical tape is still around the handle.

I crouch and run to the backside of the Yaris. I don't want to be seen. I creep around to the driver's side. It has a keypad underneath the handle. I press all the numbers, zero to nine, and nine to zero. The car alarm goes off. I run to the right side of the front door of the Yaris' front porch. I press myself hard against the bricks. I spread my arms out against the wall. I pretend I'm stuck against it, like Spiderman. It feels like that, it feels like I am stuck like a spider in a web.

The front door of the house opens. The door almost hits me in the face, it was swung open so hard. That means the person who opened it is either scared or really mad. Just my New Balance shoes show under the door. I can hear someone step on the porch. He is searching for me. He is big, and has a baseball bat. My heart beats faster. I clench the knife tighter. He's almost off the porch now. He's wearing dust and mud on his clothes. He probably works in construction. He probably made the fountain outside the gas station. I look to the left side of the door. I see him grumbling around the car. He's trying to make sure no one is sneaking up on him.

A light from the neighbor's house turns on. He needs to turn off the alarm. If he turns off the alarm, I can be cured. He drops the baseball bat. I hear it thunk the pavement. "Turn the fucking alarm off, asshole!" the neighbor yells out his window. "If you don't turn the fucking shit off, I'm coming down with my shotgun!" I hold my breath. The alarm shuts off. I breathe out and close my eyes. This is it. This is what I've been waiting for. I'm going to be cured!

I hear his baseball bat. It is rolling down the pavement. Bump, bump, bump it goes skipping down the driveway. It knocks against the wood of the first step of the porch then the second. Now the third. Now is the time. I hold my knife tighter. I jump from behind the door. I put my left hand over his mouth. I put the knife to his throat with my right.

"Don't move. Don't do anything. I don't want to hurt you. I just want the cure. We're going inside, okay?" He nods. His body stiffens. He stops. He doesn't want me to be cured. "If you struggle, I'm going to hurt you. I don't want to hurt you. I just want the cure. Open the door, and slowly."

We go inside. The carpet is forest green. Mom liked the forest. I close the door. The whole place smells like leather. "If you scream, I'll kill you. I don't want to kill you. I just want the cure."

"I don't know what you're talking about, but just tell me what you want and I'll give it to you. Just don't hurt us!" The man is crying.

"I don't know where the cure is. The Dragons will tell

me."

"I don't know what you're talking about! Just tell me what you want! Do you want money? How about jewelry? Just please, please don't hurt us!" he pleads. He swallows and his Adam's apple grazes the knife.

"Where is your wife?" I ask him.

"Uh, U-Upstairs."

"Is she awake?"

"No, she's a heavy sleeper."

"Do you have any kids?"

"Just one. Please don't hurt him. Don't fucking touch him."

"How old?"

"Fuck you!"

"I said how old?" I press my knife a little more into his neck.

"T-t-two," he squawks out. "For God sakes, don't hurt him."

"All I want is the cure." I bring the knife even closer to his skin. "And you're not going to stop me from getting it." I hear a voice speak in my ear.

"Kill him!" the voice whispers. "He wants to stop you from getting the cure. He wants you to disappear. He knows where the cure is. You must kill him!" It's The Dragons. They're back! They will tell me where the cure is.

"Do you want me to die? Do you want me to stay cursed? NO!"

"What the fuck are you talking about?" I slice his neck open with my knife. He tries to scream so I cover his mouth again. I push his head back. His blood is running down my arm. I hear his neck skin tearing. *from his neck* That's the sound of the cure! He tries biting my hand. That's not very nice! I turn him around so I can see him. I want to see him die. He needs to see what he did to me. I lick the cut on his neck. There's blood from one side of his neck to the other. He goes limp. I drop him to the floor. The blood puddles on the carpet. I like forest green carpet. I need to hurry. I grab him and drag him into the kitchen.

Something pushes me into the counter. I like granite. I hear a woman's voice from behind me.

"You motherfucker!" I put my hands behind my head. I grab the woman. I grab her hair. I like long hair. I fall down on purpose. She falls down with me. Her head hits the counter top. She doesn't let go of the knife. She twists the knife harder. It feels good. I roll over on top of her. She's still awake.

"Why do you want to kill me? What did I do to you? I just wanted the cure!" Her nose looks broke. I bet she broke it on the granite counter. I like granite. I punch her in her face. She screams. I lift her head up and slam it back down. I do it again. And again. "I need the cure!" I yell at her. I smash my elbow into her forehead. It cuts open. The blood runs into her long, pretty hair.

I grab her hair again. It's messy with blood. I lift her head up. I lick the blood off of her face. Nope, that's not the cure. I need the cure. I slam her head down to the linoleum. I hear her cranium crack. I do it again. I see the blood flowing out of her, snap, crackle, pop. Kellog's Rice Crispies. There's no sugar in Rice Crispies. She's unconscious now. I lick her blood off the floor. It's still not the cure. She tastes good though. There's sugar in her blood.

Her eyes are open. But she is dead. She looks peaceful now. She can be with her husband. They both wanted me dead. But they are dead. I pull the knife from my back. The knife is bloody. My blood is cursed. I need to find the cure.

I walk up the stairs. I like forest green. I keep my hand on the railing. I reach the top of the stairs. It's dark up here. I don't like the dark. It's not scary. I just don't like it. All I hear is the ticking from a clock. I don't see a clock but I hear it. It says Tick-tock, tick-tock, tick-tock. I need to find the cure.

I see two doors. They are on my left. There's only one door on the right. Right first. It's dark. I don't like the dark. I find the light switch. It's a bathroom. The walls have pirates on them. I like pirates. They're dirty, but they're happy. I want to be happy. The shower curtain moves. Maybe the cure is behind it. I slowly open it. No cure. There's five rubber duckies dressed up like pirates. I like pirates. I turn off the light. I don't like the dark.

First door on the left. It's already open. They must have known I was coming. The cure is probably here. It's a boys room. He likes trains and cars. I don't see him. I smell him. He's the cure. I get down on my hands and knees. I look under the bed. Nothing. Not even a bed monster. I check in the closet. Nope, no closet monsters either. I go back to the hallway. One more room left. One room. One cure.

I go in the room. It's a bedroom. It's bigger than the boys room. I hear a noise. It's crying. I get on my hands and knees. Nothing under the bed. Not even a bed monster. I open the closet. Nothing, not even a closet monster. I look at the window. I see two feet. They are sticking out. They're under the curtain. I hear the cry again. I pull back the curtains. There he is. There's my cure. The Dragons didn't lie! I hold out my hand. He looks at me. He doesn't grab my hand. I pick him up. He's struggling. I take him to the bathroom. The one with the pirates.

I put him down. I tell him to get in the bathtub. He does. He's a good boy. He must know he's the cure. I help him take off his pajamas. He has a diaper on. My bath only has two nozzles. This one has three. I turn them all on. I want all the water. It fills up fast. He sits down. His diaper is getting wet. It gets big, really big. I toss him a rubber duck. It's dressed like a pirate. He's still crying.

I grab the back of his head. His skin is so soft. I plunge it under the water. I see bubbles coming up. I like bubbles. He's squirming. He's trying to get away. He's splashing all over. Mommy told me not to splash in the tub. The bubbles stopped. His body goes limp. It's time for the cure. I drain the water. Mommy always makes me drain the water. I take his diaper off. He is all wet. I carry him to the boys room.

I lay him down on the little bed. I don't know how to start. The fingers. Maybe they're like chicken fingers. I grab his right hand. I nibble on his thumb. So soft. I bite his little thumb and it nearly comes off in my mouth. I suck the blood from his thumb. It tastes fresh. This is the best blood I've ever tasted. I want more. I bite the next finger. The bones crunch. I don't even choke on them. Young bones are soft. I grab my knife.

"What are you doing?" A voice says.

"Getting the cure," I respond.

"What did I tell you?" The Dragons said.

"What did I do wrong? I did what you wanted!"

"You drowned him. He's already dead! You know you needed to eat the child alive. You've failed me again. You know what's has to happen. You know what you must do. You must eat yourself as punishment. Drink your own cursed blood. If you're lucky, it won't kill you," The Dragon said.

"No, please! Don't make me do it! There has to be another way. There has to be! Please! I want to be cured!"

"No, this is the only way. This is what you deserve for what you've done."

The Dragons disappeared. I can't do it. I can't drink my own blood. It's cursed. I'll disappear. I don't want to disappear. I want to be cured. I pick up the boy's body. I run down the stairs. I run outside. I run down the street. I run. People are looking at me. Why are they out here? There are lights behind me. They keep following me. It's the police. Finally! They can help me find the cure. They want me to be cured. I don't like this curse.

They push me on the ground. Ow! They hit me with a stick. That hurts! Is this the cure? Did The Dragons lie? Is the pain the cure? I feel blood on my forehead. It's my blood. I taste it. It's not sweet like cereal. It's still cursed. I don't want to be cursed! They put handcuffs on me. Like in my magic set. They put me in the car. They call for an ambulance. He wasn't the cure. Where are we going? I bet they know where the cure is.

The Body of Willy Beacon

The Serial Killer was shocked and a little disappointed that the gun fired. He liked seeing people squirm, and wanted to prolong the experience. He wanted The Cannibal to hear the click of the gun more than he wanted his blood splattered across the table. "Well folks, we can get back to killing each other like civilized people," The Serial Killer joked. The guards came through the door, visibly upset by the killing. The prisoners could sense that the guards would have liked to see someone else get feasted upon.

"Hope you're happy," The Tall Guard said sarcastically. "Now he'll never find his cure."

"I think I did find his cure, Mr. Rent-A-Cop. Someone's heart exploding is a natural cure to many known and unknown diseases," The Serial Killer replied. The guards pulled The Cannibal's dead weight from out of his chair. Blood spilled out from the gaping wound in his chest, leaving a trail from where he sat at the table all the way to the door. The inmates sympathized with The Cannibal even though no one was willing to admit it. The Tall Guard took the gun from The Serial Killer, and handed it to The Terrorist.

The Terrorist

The Terrorist believed there was no point in talking. He already had enough enemies, talking wasn't going to help him. Even in this room full of sociopaths, confessing to the other inmates around the table that he was a spy and not a terrorist wasn't going to make him any allies. If they wanted the next person to single out, he was probably the easiest target. Who in the good ol' U S of A could sympathize with a known terrorist? He figured he would just sit here, and let them fight it out. He needed to strategize. He needed an easy shot that wouldn't piss anyone off. The Pacifist was the easiest target. He wouldn't want revenge. But he had to place it carefully. Someone may want to attack him for attacking the defenseless.

"Allah isn't going to make the decision for you. Where's your head at?" The Hitman asked.

"I'm sure you're the very last person who wants to be judged by their appearance," The Terrorist quipped back.

"Are you denying your Muslim faith? I'm not saying you're a bad person because of your faith. I'm just saying I think I got you pegged fairly easily, and you don't like it," he replied.

"No, of course I'm not denying it. But you know how it seems to everyone else. Just muttering the word Muslim doesn't bring about kindness as it should."

"Kindness...like on September 11th, that type of kindness?" The Innocent interrupted. He crossed his arms over his chest, the disapproval on his face evident to everyone else in the room.

"No more like the kindness Christian Europeans showed my people in the crusades. Americans are too focused on short term memory to realize Christians are the real terrorists of the world. Maybe not now, but looking throughout history, it certainly is true," The Terrorist replied.

"Man, if that ain't some bullshit! How can you even say that? Aren't you guys promised like 72 virgins or some shit for blowing yourself up?" asked The Gangster.

"This is exactly what I'm talking about, that's just a misconception. The Koran teaches that it's a major sin to commit suicide, not something to be celebrated and rewarded."

"Yeah right! That's what you say to save face. But you can't deny that they're the same kind of fuckers just like you, believing in the same shit, and blowing themselves up for your God Allah," said The Serial Killer.

"Maybe you are right, but there's just as many Christians blowing up doctor's offices because they don't believe in abortion. The difference is that you can't have a war on terror when Christians are the bad guys," said The Terrorist.

"No...I suppose you can't." The Innocent was silent,

the disgust on his face lessening. He was contemplating what The Terrorist just said.

"It's all just a matter of what you think is evil, and it's usually someone who's skin color is different than your own," The Terrorist continued.

"I suppose that makes sense, but it still doesn't make what your guys did right, does it?" The Innocent questioned.

"'Your guys' meaning my fellow citizens from Cincinnati?" The Terrorist asked.

"You know what I mean," answered The Innocent. He hesitated for a moment.

"No one is questioning Muhammad Ali as a terrorist because he's Muslim. Why me? What's the difference between him and me?" The Spy asked.

"Well, maybe because you're in an execution room sentenced to death by a jury of your peers for doing some fucked up shit," said The Hitman.

"Muhammad Ali beat the shit out of people for a living. It's not that much different," The Terrorist pleaded.

"I never beat anyone up, never killed anyone, and yet I am still here among you all."

"Muhammad Ali was also an inspiration to people. He may not have been a military man, but he still fought for our country just the same. He gave us something to root for," said The Innocent, once again interested in the conversation.

"I feel like I did the same for my people," The Terrorist replied.

"You mean your people from Cincinnati?" The Innocent smirked, knowing that he had cornered The Terrorist. The Terrorist kept silent. It dawned on him that no matter how hard he tried to justify his faith, what The Innocent said was true. His religion meant more to him than his country did. A cold silence blanketed the room.

An echo sounded, bouncing off the concrete walls of the execution room. The repeated tapping of a fingernail against the metal table, in perfect rhythm, pierced the silence, irritating the inmates.

"Hey, can you stop that please. Some of us are trying to kill each other here." The Serial Killer glanced at The Woman. She rolled her eyes.

"Can you be serious for like ten minutes, or are you just *that* big of an asshole?" She shot back.

"I could say I could give it an honest shot, but I'm not a liar, just a cold blooded killer. Oh, and a pervert for good measure," The Serial Killer laughed.

"Say whatever you want. It doesn't make you any less of a disgusting shit head!" The Woman replied.

"It doesn't get me any farther away from getting a shot inside your pants either," The Serial Killer said.

"I do not believe my religion would allow me to kill

someone who would not be able and willing to kill me, nor would it allow me to kill a woman. You are the only one I would feel right about giving the honor to," The Terrorist said. He cocked the hammer back on the gun, and pointed at The Hitman, giving him a slight nod.

"I understand and accept the honor," The Hitman said. He proudly stood, and held his hands behind his back as if he were in the presence of royalty. "If you're going to kill me, I want to be sure you execute me. I will never allow myself to be gunned down unknowingly." The Terrorist placed his finger around the trigger.

-Click-

The Innocent

The Terrorist placed the gun down and like a bartender in a grungy bar in Mexico, slid the gun quickly across the table. The Innocent wasn't expecting it. The Innocent quickly placed his hands over where he thought the gun was going to land. He missed. Instead It fell into his lap. He looked down, and picked it up with one hand around the barrel. "So is that how you jerked off all the men at the glory hole?" The Innocent didn't even bother to look up. He knew it was The Serial Killer who made the smart-ass remark.

"Yeah it is. Your mom taught me everything she knows," The Innocent said.

"So you have met her. Okay then, Jock-O Mallone, who are you gonna take out this time?" The Serial Killer jabbed.

"You gonna try for the black guy again? Maybe this time it'll stick, so it'll just be us whiteys around here. Well except for you, Ahmed, but you know what they say: if you're not white, you're black." The Terrorist couldn't help but smile at the remark.

"Well, it's certainly good knowing what side I'm on," The Terrorist replied.

"Hey now, let's not get hasty. You're still a terrorist, but at least you have a sense of humor, albeit shallow as the water in your deserts," The Serial Killer said.

"Thanks."

"Anytime. So who's it going to be, boy?" The Serial Killer asked.

"I don't want to kill anyone. I'm not like you all. I don't enjoy this," said The Innocent.

"You think I enjoy this?" The Woman remarked. "This is fucking terrible. Sitting around knowing we're all fucked, and knowing while our family is grieving our deaths, some sociopath is rejoicing with theirs. How am I supposed to enjoy that?"

"I just wish so fucking bad that we were in Washington State. They just let them go, and gave them a second chance at life. I bet none of those lucky motherfuckers kill again. I have to kill if I want to make it out of here alive. That's what's fucked up. We all want the same thing, but even killing isn't good enough to get us out of here. You have to be the last one alive."

"It's pretty fucked up, though, the thing that put us into this shit-hole situation is the only way we have to get out of it," The Gangster said. "I mean we kill, get thrown in prison, just so they can kill us? Just so we can kill each other to be set free? What kind of damn sense does any of that make?"

"That's a quandary that has plagued man since biblical times. How do you kill a killer without becoming one yourself?" The Pacifist replied. "In the middle ages, they had an executioner. It was a job you applied for. You wore a mask to hide your face so none of the family members could seek revenge on you, but more than that, you were celebrated as an icon of justice. People looked up to the executioner. It's different now. They treat executions like a medical procedure. You don't even get to know if you were the one that executed the prisoner. Even with a firing squad, there's one gunman shooting blanks just so all five shooters can go home at night, not feeling guilty about being the person who executed the prisoner. That should be proof enough that it's wrong. Why should they feel guilty if they all knew it was the right thing to do?"

"What about lethal injections? Don't they just have one person injecting that shit into you?" The Innocent asked.

"Lethal injection is especially muddled in that respect. The physician hooks up the IV with three different chemicals, only one of which contains the Potassium Chloride which actually stops your heart. The other two put you to sleep. They have a different lab technician administer a different drug, so again, they can go home at night and think they just gave the inmate the barbiturate to put them asleep."

~~The Innocent leans forward continuing his speech.~~ "The quandary is," The Innocent said, _leaning forward_ "that these people are certified lab technicians. They know exactly which drug is which. If they didn't, they wouldn't be able to administer it with the correct dosage. It's the fact they are told they aren't guilty that they don't feel guilty."

"So what is it you are saying? What's the fucking point?" The Gangster asked.

"The point is, we've already concluded as a country that we should feel guilty for murder, regardless of the actions that person committed. There shouldn't be a death penalty. We should have to repay our debt to society, of course, but killing us only makes someone else a murderer," The Innocent said. The buzzer went off.

"Well, regardless how I feel about any of you here, I'd rather not piss anyone else off." The Innocent raised the gun and aimed at The Gangster.

"Ah, shit man! Really? Ain't gonna give me a fucking break for a minute, are ya? Well, whatever man. Just get on with it," The Gangster said.

The Innocent cocked back the hammer confidently. There was no one laughing at him this time. "Please don't let me become a murderer," The Innocent prayed to himself. He closed his eyes and pulled the trigger.

R.L. Murphy

-Click-

The Pacifist

The Innocent passed the gun to The Pacifist. "Alright fellas, we can relax once again," The Serial Killer said. The Pacifist picked a bullet from the pile on the table. He watched The Serial Killer while he loaded the third bullet into the gun and snapped the chamber shut.

"Just because I have no intention of killing anyone around this table doesn't mean you get off easy. I still have the only power in the room, whether you like it or not," The Pacifist replied.

"But everyone knows you ain't gonna do shit with it, man," The Gangster said.

"Does that really matter? I still have the choice. You know I could. No one knows what anyone else is going to do. I'm in here for a reason. Everyone has a relapse every once in a while," The Pacifist said.

"So you're going to sit here and lecture us for the next ten minutes? That sounds great," The Woman said. "You really know how to keep a woman entertained."

"Well, I guess you're just looking at it the wrong way. Even if you get nothing out of me mentoring you, it beats the alternative of me having a decent shot of killing one of you."

"Don't be so sure about that, Buddha. I'd rather eat a

bullet than hear you ramble on and on about our 'souls' and 'enlightenment' for another ten minutes," said The Serial Killer.

"Why do preachers do last rites when they know we're going to hell? Notice they've dropped that formality here with us. It's because we all want to believe that even though we've committed atrocities, we still want to believe our souls can be saved," The Pacifist preached.

"Really? Do any of us really think that we will be saved? Hey Ahmed, you going to see those virgins? Hey Gangster G, have you made your reservations yet? 'Sup Whore, who's cock are you going to suck on first in heaven?" The Serial Killer jabbed.

"Fuck you, you smug fuck!" The Woman gave him the finger. "One of us has to make it out of here alive. That's the whole point to this fucked up game. So what the fuck do you care if we keep hope? Why do you care so much?"

"It makes me laugh to think that you guys think any of us are really getting out of here alive. We think we're good people, but we're not. Can you imagine if we did get out of here, what kind of Texas sized shit storm the media will have? On top of that, we live in goddamn Texas. There are a million people waiting for a chance to kill us. We would become bums, and we'd probably be better off dead anyway. Well, except you," The Serial Killer said pointing to The Terrorist. "

You would probably have no problem going back to

your home country and being considered a hero."

"Don't pretend to care about us because you don't. You simply want to capitalize on our dreams, the dreams that you're crushing. Whoever wins will have a difficult life, but it's better than prison, and it's certainly better than death," The Pacifist said. The buzzer sounded.

The Pacifist grabbed the gun, pointed it in the air, and said, "We're all going to die, but today one of us gets to live."

-Click-

The Woman

The Pacifist passed the gun to The Woman. She picked it up, feeling the weight of the power in her hand and poked open the cylinder with her finger. "Three bullets down, three to go," The Woman said as she placed the fourth bullet into the chamber and flipped it shut. "Hmmm," she pondered, "now which one of you assholes do I want to take out? Oh I wonder, hmmm...."The Woman tapped the barrel of the gun against her temple.

"Okay, okay, c'mon now, we all know your pussy's wet for me. The thought of my blood on your face makes your nipples hard. Why do you gotta rub it in?" said The Serial Killer.

"Because it's fun, and you know it's coming, no reason to hide it. You're a mother fucker and you know it, you take pride in it," said The Woman.

"I know, but don't act like I'm the only asshole here. Look around, I'm just the one who's not fake about it. I'll tell you I'm an asshole. I'll tell you I want you dead, these peckers are too concerned with getting out of here to do that. Not I, said the fly," said The Serial Killer.

"Maybe that's true, but it doesn't make you any less of an asshole. You'd be the same asshole if you were in here or not," said The Woman.

"Yeah, that's about the milk and skinny of it, I'm not afraid to die my dear little jizm princess, I'm already dead. I know you're about to kill me and I'm okay with it. I'm just trying to have a good time until it happens, is that so bad? I hope you pull that trigger and that bullet goes right through my forehead. I want the blood to splatter so hard that the pigs watching us need a ladder to clean skull fragments from the ceiling. I'm not suicidal; I just don't want to go out like one of the whores I killed," The Serial Killer said.

"Well lucky for you, you're getting your wish. Maybe I should shoot your dick off instead, Would you like that? How about I don't kill you? How about I just shoot you somewhere that won't kill you, just make you feel pain you miserable fuck?" The Woman said.

"Why are you thinking about my dick so much? I would let you suck it, but I'm fresh out of twenty dollar bills," The Serial Killer said as he pantomimed fellatio with his hand and mouth. The buzzer went off.

"You know very God damn well I'm not a fucking whore,"

"Kurt Vonnegut once said 'Every woman is a whore, you just have to know her price.' While I don't completely agree, it is the main emotional difference between men and women; men have pride while women will do anything they think is necessary to survive," said The Pacifist. Everyone stared at him surprised he had entered the immature conversation.

"See even the brainiac thinks you're a whore. Maybe that's just because his dick is closer to you than mine," The Serial Killer said then continued with his pantomime.

"No, that's not what I meant at all, but I appreciate the sarcasm," said The Pacifist.

"God, can I just shoot you now?" said The Woman.

"Nothing stopping you but your weak woman hands," The Serial Killer said. The Woman lifted her arms and pointed the gun at her target.

"Go to hell cock sucker!" The Woman said ~~as she~~ pulling the trigger.

-Click-

The Hitman

The Woman felt defeated by the cold, sharp sound of the click the gun made. She slouched back in her chair disappointed, thinking for sure The Serial Killer would be dead. Instead she slid the gun across the table towards The Hitman.

The Hitman opened the cylinder of the gun and grabbed a bullet from the pile in the middle of the table, placing it in one of the two remaining slots. The Hitman flicked his wrist, snapping the barrel shut. The tension in the air was thick. Everyone around the table was open to target. This shot was almost a guaranteed kill. The Terrorist cleared his throat, and broke the silence.

"Just because you don't agree with my religion shouldn't be a reason to kill me."

"Actually it sounds like a perfect reason to me," The Serial Killer said laughing.

"Religious intolerance is at the root of the majority of war," said The Pacifist.

"Man, you always have my back. I guess even pacifists hate terrorists," said The Serial Killer.

"There's no use in debating this, I already know who I'm killing. It has nothing to do with my own personal feelings against anyone. The person who wants me dead is who I'm going to kill. It's as simple as that," The Hitman stated.

"And you're not going to tell us who it is until the buzzer goes off, are you?" The Woman asked.

"No," The Hitman said.

"Well, I guess we just sit back until one of us is gone," said The Woman.

"And since you already made up your mind, we can say anything about you and it won't affect your decision," said The Serial Killer.

"I wouldn't be so sure. There's always the next round. I wouldn't be so quick to make me an enemy," The Hitman said.

"So you think there's only one main threat to you in this room?" The Innocent asked him.

"I think there is one person at this table who would kill us all if he is not taken care of immediately," The Hitman said.

"I guess I'm safe for a little bit longer," said The Pacifist relieved.

"If you think for one moment that I don't see through your bullshit, you're delusional," replied The Hitman to The Pacifist. "You're pretending to pose no threat to us so that no one feels they need to take you out...that is until you realize it's time to strike. I can see straight through your game. You're not a pacifist, you're a viper."

"I can see your point, but I'm going to die in this room. I will not commit another act of violence on another human being or animal," said The Pacifist.

"Wait, wait, wait! So you're a vegetarian too? What did you order for your last meal, parsnips and celery with a side order of cock in your mouth?" The Innocent quipped.

"Just because I choose not to murder for my meals doesn't mean I am a homosexual," The Pacifist said.

"I'm not saying that all vegetarians are queer. I'm just saying if you've eaten tofu you've probably had a dick in your mouth," said The Serial Killer.

"Man, that whole 'not eatin' meat' thing is a complete whitey thing. Not a single person in the hood that don't eat meat," said The Gangster.

"That probably has much to do with genetics. The majority of Africans two hundred years ago hunted their own food. Very little farming can be done in such a harsh environment," said The Pacifist.

"I didn't know they had chicken in Africa," The Innocent replied. "So what would you have for your last meal?"

"Well, I'd have my mom make me her ribs, with cornbread, and corn on the cob. No better meal in this world, you know?" said The Gangster. The buzzer sounded. "And Funyuns, I love those things."

"I'm sorry you won't get to enjoy it," The Hitman said. He raised his gun, aiming it at The Gangster.

-Bang-

The Story of George Campbell

"Why must I be evil to provide for my family?"

My alarm clock goes off. I've been staring at the red numbers flashing on its face for the last ten minutes. Why didn't I just get up when I woke up a half hour ago, who the hell knows? It's time to start off another day. I roll out of my futon and get dressed.

I knock on Tyler's door instead of just opening it. The damn boy needs to get over this whole "I hate being surprised" thing. "Son, wake up," I say outside his door. "You gotta get up for school. You don't want to be late for Mrs. Monica's class again."

"Okay Dad, gimme a few more minutes," Tyler mumbles. I open the door and sit down on his bed. I lay my hand on his shoulder and give him a nudge. He turns away from me, wrapping himself tighter in his Transformers blanket.

"You got one minute Tyler, and don't make me have to come back to get you," I say. He still hasn't taken well to the adjustment. Who can blame him? Neither have I. It's hard to adapt to this life after his mother, the love of my life, walked out, no note or nothin'. She left me to take care of our boy on my own. When he was born and she nestled his little body close to her for the very first time, never in my wildest dreams did I imagine this would happen. I miss her. I hope Tyler never finds out where she went or why she left. Maybe someday she'll get clean and come back to us.

I make my way downstairs and turn on the overhead light in the kitchen. There, scurrying across the floor like it owns the damned house, is a cockroach crawling from underneath the dishwasher and into my motherfucking water heater room. Goddamn it, I thought we got rid of those nasty things! I keep the kitchen clean as shit but I can only get rid of them for a couple weeks before the nasty ass things come crawling back. Another is crawling near the refrigerator. I crush it with my barefoot.

I grab a small bowl out of the cupboard, looking to make sure there aren't any cockroaches crawling around my dishware. I set it on the table in the middle of the kitchen. I grab the last spoon out of the drawer. It seems out of place, being smaller than the rest of my silverware. Why the hell haven't I just thrown it away? It makes a small clink as I toss it in the bowl. I've always loved the sound a spoon makes in a bowl.

I grab the box of Sugar Puffs from the top of the refrigerator, and pour what's left of it into the bowl. I fill the bowl it with milk, watching the cereal as it floats to the top. "Boy, your breakfast is ready! You need to get down here!" I yell up the stairs.

A muffled voice yells back, "Ay bwushin mah teef."

"Alright, just hurry it up." I strap on my boots while I wait. I throw my black ski mask down on the table as I hear Tyler stomp down the stairs.

"What's that for dad?" He points to the mask as he sits down in his char to eat breakfast.

"Skiing, what do you think? Mind your own business and don't ask so many questions. Now, eat your cereal. You're going to be late for school if you don't hurry. The bus will be here any minute," I say to him. I watch as he takes two more bites of cereal and rushes out the door, his backpack slung around one arm.

As soon as I hear the back door slam shut, I pull out the checklist I made of the things I need for today. The list goes like this:

1. Durable cloth bag. Check.

2. Ski mask. Check

3. Shoebox with wallet in it. Check

4. One hundred dollars cash in a clip. Check

5. Gun with two extra clips. Check

6. Leather gloves. Check

I unzip the Duffle Bag on the floor, being diligent to place the rest of the shit in it. I lay the filled Duffle Bag down next to the back door and wait. I go over the plan a million times in my head. I hear a distant horn honk outside. It's go time. I grab the bag, step outside and lock my door.

Jimmy's Dodge Charger is parked in front of my house. I get in the passenger backseat and lay the bag across my lap. The rest of the gang is here. They stay silent while Jimmy sings along to a song playing on the radio. I watch the scenery as we drive to our destination. Ten minutes later we arrive.

Jimmy goes over me the plan with me one last time. I'm on crowd control duty, Jimmy's the bag man, Jason is on cop and camera duty, and his bitch Gina is the driver. My stomach drops while Jimmy is discussing our strategy. I think this may be a big mistake. I have a fucking kid, what the hell am I thinking? I can't go through with this.

"Put your masks on, we're going in two minutes," Jimmy says as he pulls out his gun. Each second that passes feels like an eternity. "Guns loaded and safety off in one minute," Jimmy says.

The only time I've used a gun is when Jimmy had me go to the shooting range with him. I've only been out there twice with him. I had pretty good aim considering my lack of experience. There's something about holding a gun in your hand that makes you feel powerful. It feels like you have the power of God in your hand. You get to decide who lives and who dies. Sometimes it's the only control people have in their lives. Jimmy is one of those people.

I remember when I was thirteen and Jimmy brought his dad's glock to school. That's when I knew he was batshit crazy. He pointed the thing (gun) at me pretending to shoot me, the asshole. If Jimmy ever found out I was the one that ratted him out, he'd blow my brains out.

"Alright, masks on," Jimmy says. The anxiety is unbearable. I've never committed a felony. What the fuck is going to happen to my kid if I get caught, or worse, fucking killed? I can't afford to get caught. Jimmy's a dumb motherfucker and we let *him* make this plan? We're so fucked. This is a big fucking mistake. I need to bail.

"George, put your fucking mask on! I said it's fucking go time!" I pull my mask over my face. All three of us step out of Jimmy's car at the same moment. I can't do this. My heart is beating so fast I swear it's going to explode in my chest. I can't hear what Jimmy and Jason are saying. Fuck it, life is a gamble. I'm already here and my kid deserves a better life than the one he has.

I walk through the double doors that lead into the lobby of this bank. I've never seen such thick glass in my life. This place is fucking beautiful. Everything is made out of either glass or marble and everything sparkles. I've never encountered such a luxurious bank.

"Wake up, nigga'," Jimmy says as he shoves me on the shoulder. When I look around, I notice everyone is staring at us, bewildered by the event that is happening. Without hesitation, Jimmy runs toward the tellers. Jason has the two guards kneeling on the floor with their hands over their heads. My job is to keep any bystanders from trying to be a hero so Jimmy, Jason, and myself can get out of this alive. I've talked plenty of people out of shooting Jimmy in the past. This is just another one of those times. I grab my gun and point it in the air.

"Look," I yell. My voice echoes off the pristine walls of this building. "We know what it's like to get robbed. We're only here to get our goddamn money this greedy ass institution stole from us, from you! Don't you see? All they want to do is nothing more than to charge you fees. Fees for over drafting, fees because you used the wrong ATM, fees to just hold onto your own goddamn money. It's a goddamn scam!"

I take a deep breath. "When I walked in here all I saw was how goddamn nice this place is. How do you think they got the money for all of this shit?" I spread my arms, careful to aim my gun in the air and away from the bystanders, and spin around, displaying the richness of the lobby. "Do you think marble is cheap? They got the money for all this from you and me. They stole that money from us. We're not the bad guys here. We're just tired of getting ripped off by fucking corporate businesses that say they have our best interests at heart. So sit back and let us do what we got to do. The sooner we finish, the sooner you get to go on with your day."

I see someone move from the corner of my eye. I turn around and watch as an old, white man in a tan cowboy hat is whispering to a Latina woman next to him. Something tells me that he has a gun. He's going to try to be a fucking hero, I can feel it.

"Hey you!" I point my gun at the old man's face. I can see the sweat rolling down from his brow, soaking into his collar as I confront him. "If you even think you're going to play the hero here, I'll make sure to blow your pretty little cracker brain all over these beautiful, clean white walls. I don't want to hurt you but if you're gonna act dumb, I can make sure it happens."

I see that Jason has already disarmed the security cameras, just like we planned. He has some sort of device that looks like it's straight out of the movies that blocks all wireless signals from going in and out. As long as this contraption is on, there is no cell phone service in or out, and neither can the alarms sound. I see Jimmy holding the bag open and the teller, a pretty little girl in a yellow blouse, is throwing stacks of cash in it. Jimmy's nervous. He looks like he's getting ready to pull the trigger in the teller's face.

The lobby is filled with an odd silence. I can sense how terrified the people are. Scared of us, and scared of me. Jimmy yells back at us, "Okay, we're good." He backs away from the counter, careful not to turn his back, with the cash spilling out from the bag. He continues to aim the gun at the teller's head.

"Okay everyone, we'll be out of your hair in a flash," Jimmy says. Two gun shots fire from outside the building. Jimmy looks at me and I'm just as surprised by the sound as he is. Jason looks at the door. We hear glass shatter as three more gunshot blasts ring throughout the building. *[handwritten: entrance] [handwritten: rework this] [handwritten: Door is got shattered in the main of chapter]*

Jason pushes up against the wall beside the glass doors. I watch as he peeks outside, the door to assess our situation. "Motherfuckin' cops!" he yells at us. There are three more shots outside and more yelling. I look around the room. Everyone's scared, even Jimmy. Two more shots go off. I draw my gun towards the door.

"Pigs aren't fucking around out there. They shot Gina right in her fucking head. Those goddamn motherfuckers!" Jason yells.

"Jason, what's happening? Why the fuck are the cops here?" I ask. Jason reaches into his backpack and pulls out the cell blocker.

"Shit, shit, shit! I didn't turn it on. I'm sorry! I didn't turn the motherfucking thing on," Jason says.

"You dumb motherfucker! You just got us fucking killed," Jimmy screams. "What the fuck are we going to do now? We can't just walk the fuck out of here. And you best fucking believe I ain't going to prison over your stupid ass! This is fucking bullshit and it's all your fucking fault!" Jimmy points his gun at Jason.

"C'mon Jimmy! There's no reason to fucking shoot me over this shit," Jason says. There is no reasoning with Jimmy. Why the fuck did we even do this? I should have told him to fuck off when he asked if I wanted in on this ordeal. The things people do for money. The things people do for their family.

Jimmy is yelling at the teller in the yellow blouse. He shoves his gun in her face. He's trying to scare her into admitting that she was the one who pushed the emergency button under the counter. "Shooting innocent people isn't going to get us out of here," I say trying to stop Jimmy from making another mistake. Jimmy nods in agreement with me, and then pulls the trigger into the teller's skull. Her blood splashes in every direction as her body slumps over the counter.

"Here's an idea," Jimmy says, "let's kill all of these cocksuckers." Jimmy aims his gun towards the two guards. The tension in the air is thick with fear and insanity.

"You're not killing anyone else! We got to get the fuck out of here," I say.

"I already killed the teller, dumb shit! Don't you see we're already fucked?" Jimmy laughs. Jimmy walks over to one of the guards and kicks him in his side. The guard doubles over, and vomits. "Was it you? Are you the fucker who called the fucking Police? It was you, wasn't it?" Jimmy kicks him again. The guard falls face forward into his own puke. "You wanted to be the hero, didn't ya? Think you're a big fucking man now?

You're just a fucking pussy," Jimmy says, putting the barrel of the gun to the back of the man's head.

"Please don't," The guard cries, puke dripping down the side of his face.

"Jimmy, calm the fuck down! You're not a fucking cop killer," I say.

"This motherfucker isn't a cop, he's a fucking security guard," Jimmy says as he pulls the trigger. "Motherfucking Rent-A-Cop is all he could ever aim to be!" Jimmy spits on the remains of the security guard's head.

"You dumb motherfucker! What the fuck do you think you're doing? Do you think they couldn't hear that outside? We're so fucking dead, Jimmy. We're all dead because of your goddamn dumb ass!" I say. I'm starting to lose my cool. I see the old man in the cowboy hat reach for his gun. Jimmy sees this too and doesn't hesitate to plant a bullet in his head. The ringing of the gunshot blends in with the screams of the other people in the lobby. Things are spinning out of control.

"Jimmy, stop you crazy fuck!" I yell, hoping that Jimmy can hear me.

"What the fuck do you care? We're all dead anyways. I'm not going to be gunned down by some old honky bastard trying to be the hero," Jimmy says. I have to make a decision if I want to make it out of here alive. Jimmy's got to be stopped by any means. I raise the gun I am holding in Jimmy's direction.

"Jimmy, you need to stop!" I aim the gun at his head.

"What the fuck do you think you are doing?" Jimmy aims his own weapon at me. "Whose fucking side are you on?" The remaining security guard backs himself into the corner behind Jimmy. Jimmy doesn't notice the movement. He's preoccupied with the thought of killing me before I kill him. He doesn't give a shit that I have a kid to take care of. He doesn't care that I'm the only real fucking friend he has ever had.

I pull the trigger and Jimmy does the same. I feel the bullet from his gun clip my ear. Jimmy is still standing, I missed. Ah shit, I didn't miss, I just missed Jimmy. The security guard behind Jimmy is holding his neck, blood spurting out between his fingers. Jimmy raises his gun again. I can't move. The security guard falls to the ground while the blood from his neck covers the floor underneath him. This is all too surreal. Another shot goes off. My arms shield my face but I don't feel anything this time. Jimmy falls to his knees, his face smashing onto the tiled floor.

I turn around to see Jason with his gun raised where Jimmy was standing. "You crazy motherfucker," Jason says. Jason isn't looking well. Blood is quickly spreading over his clothing around his shoulder. He must have gotten shot from the earlier gun fire. He needs medical attention now or he's not going to make it. The glass door cracks open. Someone from outside rolls a small white can into the middle of the lobby. It explodes in a blinding light, leaving my ears ringing in its wake.

A flood of footsteps come running through the glass doors. I hear the voices of men yelling as they get closer to me but I can't see anyone. Another gunshot rings through the smoky air. Before I know it, there's someone grabbing my wrist. They shove me to the ground. I can't see who it is. I am being dragged across the floor. They flip me over onto my stomach as cold metal wraps around my wrists. There are knees in my back doing their best to hold me down.

My vision begins to return. I can see the faint outline of someone in the smoke as I lay on my stomach. The person in front of me is kneeling. I nudge closer to the figure until it becomes clear. It's Jason. I call out his name. There's no response. He was in no condition to make a run for it. But I was hoping that he could still survive this mess. I am losing hope that he will survive. From within the smoke, I can make out a tiny gleam of light coming through a hole in the middle of his head. My heart drops to my stomach. They killed him. They executed a man who was already wounded while he was on his fucking knees. I know how this story is going to end. They're going to execute me next.

I jerk my body hard enough to throw the men holding me down away from me. I force myself up and run towards the light that I see shining through the smoke. The light must lead to the entrance of the building. I reach the door and throw my body through the glass. All I can make out are red and blue lights, and the constant whirl of sirens. I try my best to run away from the commotion, but in the end I hear the stomp of footsteps and voices catching up behind me. I faintly hear the word "stop", but nothing else.

I hit something hard that nearly stops me in my tracks. I keep going. The voices seem to be farther away now. The more I run, the clearer my vision becomes. Car horns are honking at me. I must be in the street. Fuck it, these cars aren't going to stop me. I got to get out of here.

Another gunshot rings through the air. I fall to the ground as my leg feels like it's being ripped from my body. They got me in my motherfucking leg. I stand up and try to continue running. I can't move nearly as fast and I'm sure there's a blood trail behind me, but I have to keep going. Another shot rings through the air and I fall again. It's harder now to catch my breath. The back of my shirt is wet, and I can't tell if it's blood or if it's sweat. Struggling through the pain, I manage to get back up. I stumble forward. The voices are closing in on me. My chest seizes up, making it hard to breathe. It knocks me to my knees. I stand up again, the adrenaline pushing me forward. Another shot goes off. There is screaming all around me.

This is my last chance to escape. I need to do this for me, for my kid. I try to take a deep breath but the pain in my chest prevents me from getting a good breath in.

I am pushed to the ground from behind. Someone turns me over and I look into the face of the pig that knocked me down. It's a woman in plain clothes. She's a goddamn pedestrian. I try to stand up again but she pushes me back down, pinning me down this time with her hands on my shoulders.

Moments later the police arrive, more out of breath than I am.

"We got you, you cocksucker," one of the officers says.

"You got us a long time ago," I said.

"Whatever the fuck that means," the officer replies. He motions to one of his colleagues, telling him to call for medical assistance. "I should let you die here on the street, asshole. You don't deserve to live, you know that? I'm going to make sure your black ass fries in the chair for what you've done."

"Fuck you, cocksucker! I did it for my boy, my motherfucking boy," I say. The medics arrive. They uncuff me and strap me down to the gurney.

"Your boy don't have you now, son. He's better off without you," the officer taunts me while I am loaded into the ambulance. I guess he's right, my son is better off without me. I failed him as a father and a man. Today I have lost my freedom, my child, and my life.

The Body of George Campbell

Blood squirted out of the hole in George Campbell's neck as he slumped back in his chair. His heart was still hard at work pumping the blood from within his body out through the wound as George fought for his life. He stared at The Hitman, pleading with his eyes for help. George wrapped his hands around the hole left by the gunshot blast hoping to stop the blood from pouring out of him. The force of his still beating heart pumped the blood between his fingers.

The Woman couldn't help but shut her eyes from the horror and turned away. The sound of a desperate man gasping for those last breaths of air echoed throughout the room, bouncing off the concrete walls and tattooed within the minds of the remaining six inmates. Like a wounded dog hit by a car, George knew he was a goner but he had no other choice but to wait for death's embrace. George tried to take another breath, deep and rattling, but with each wheezing of each breath he took became louder and more unbearable.

Finally the horrific sound ceased, and George's hands, soaked with his blood, dropped to his sides. His head hit the table, shaking the inmates to their very core. The slow drip of blood out of the wound on George's neck puddled onto the tile floor, tap, tap, tap. The monotonous sound was driving The Woman over the edge.

"Somebody make it stop!" she cried out. "Please just take him out of here. He's dead now, okay? I can't take any more of this!" Tears managed to escape her tightly clenched eyes, slipping down her cheeks and staining her orange jumpsuit. The door opened. The three guards walked through.

"I guess this was some sort of hate crime, right boys? Room full of white guys taking out all the darkies. Can't say I blame you, really," The Tall Guard remarked as he rolled George out of his chair, leaving his body at the feet of The Terrorist. The Terrorist shuddered in disgust. The Short Guard knelt down behind George's body and wrapped his arms around him as if he were giving him the Heimlich. He looked up at The Terrorist and said, "I got a feeling you're next. You're the darkest one left." The guards laughed at the remark as they dragged the body of George Campbell to the door. All that was left behind was the trail of bloody footprints made by the guards, that resembled some sort footprints made by a blood monster. When the door finally shut, The Woman opened her eyes, still wet and salty with fresh tears. The Hitman emptied the contents from the barrel of the gun, throwing the unused bullets back into the pile of bullets on the table, and handed the now empty weapon to The Serial Killer.

The Serial Killer

The Serial Killer grabbed the gun *from the Hitman* and opened the cylinder with a flick of his wrist. He took a bullet from the pile, placed it in the empty chamber, and let out a loud sigh. He was annoyed about his shot. "What's wrong?" The Woman mocked, "Somebody cranky and needs a nap?" She smiled, her pouty lips teasing the *remaining* inmates.

"I won't be able to sleep well until I know you're sucking cock up in hell, babe," The Serial Killer remarked. "Every time, every single goddamn time it's my turn, it's never a threat. There's always only *one* a bullet or two in the damn thing. It's like having a giant dick that never blows a load, what's the point in having it?"

"Well, what's the point in your small dick that never ejaculates?" The Innocent said, obviously proud of his quip.

"Yeah, what was the deal with that? I read in some reports that you never left any semen inside any of the women that you killed. Couldn't finish the job?" The Woman asked with a *glowing* mile-wide smirk on her face.

"That made-for-TV movie they put out was total bullshit. They just didn't want me to come off looking like the superhero that I am. I never fucked sluts like you did, whore. I don't need to rape them. I just wanted to kill them. Sorry that I break the 'whore killing' stereotype," The Serial Killer said leaning back in his chair.

"I bet half the girls you did fuck wished you had killed them," The Woman replied.

"You're just all a bunch of fucking jokers, aren't ya? I'll have you know I got around quite a bit. Never while I was married for obvious reason, but I did have a certain reputation," The Serial Killer said. He stuck his tongue out, slowly moving it back and forth across his lips.

"Cute, real cute," The Innocent interrupted. "But wait, what? You never cheated on your wife?"

"I may be a son of a bitch, but I'm an honest son of a bitch. Sex was never that big of a deal to me. I could always get it. I just had to make sure I married someone who enjoyed it as much as I did," The Serial Killer replied.

"What happened?" The Innocent asked.

"The bitch cheated on me. I guess my cock was too much for her to handle," The Serial Killer snickered.

"What about you? You ever 'go astray'?" The Serial Killer asked The Woman.

"I was with a man once who thought our relationship was more serious than I did, but that was it. I'm a fairly loyal person," The Woman said.

"Poor guy. How did you break it to him?" The Innocent asked.

"I didn't," The Woman said. "He got the point when he

saw me on a date with another guy. I knew I crushed his heart, and I really did like him, just not as much as he liked me. I was eighteen. I was just out to have fun, nothing serious."

"How would you have felt to have been that guy?" The Pacifist confronted her. "Can you imagine seeing someone you really liked with someone else? The person you probably had feelings for, perhaps for a long time? And right when you think your dream is about to come true, you find her in someone else's arms."

"I try not to think about it like that, but it's still his fault anyway. I didn't make him like me," The Woman said.

"But you knew that he did, and you still took advantage of him," said The Pacifist.

"There's nothing wrong with it, per se, but it's definitely not a nice thing to do."

"Maybe so, but I was young. It was just stupid high school stuff," The Woman remarked. "Bleh! This is boring! Let's talk about get back to last meals. So Akbar, since you're being your usual quiet self, we'll start with you. What divinely inspired Middle Eastern dish would you have for your last meal?" The Serial Killer asked.

"I couldn't really tell you. I'm from Cincinnati and the only cuisine we're known for is chili with spaghetti in it," said The Terrorist.

"Wait, what?" The Innocent remarked confused.

"Really? You guys put spaghetti in your chili? That's about as un-American as it gets."

"I never said I liked it. I only said it's the only dish native to 'my land'."

"So spill it. What would you have for your last meal?" asked The Innocent.

"I don't think I'd want anything. I don't want to shit my pants after I die. I know when I'm dead it won't matter, but at the same time I don't want to create a mess for anyone," The Terrorist said.

"Fuck that shit! Those pigs deserve to clean up every last piece of corn shit stuck to my pants," The Innocent said.

"But that's just the thing," The Terrorist said. "It's probably not the guard who's doing it. It almost has to be some guy they hire just to clean the shit up. It's probably some sort of minimum wage gig where the only good days are when they don't have a last meal."

"Fuck them though. If they didn't want to clean up shit, they shouldn't have taken the job," The Innocent said.

The buzzer rang.

"Hey, guess it's time to try and kill another one of you whores. Here's the good news, honey," The Serial Killer said while waving the gun in The Woman's face. "If this gun does go off, it certainly wouldn't be the first shot in the mouth you've ever taken."

"Fuck y..."

-Click-

The Terrorist

The Serial Killer stuck his tongue out at The Woman and slid the gun to The Terrorist. "I bet you've taken more shots in the mouth than me, asshole!" The Woman said. The Terrorist opened the chamber and placed a bullet in.

"Oh, let me guess, you tell all the guys you're blowing that 'you're allergic?'" The Innocent mocked.

"What's with you? Been rejected from throat sex one too many times there, partner?" The Serial Killer asked.

"Once is too many," The Innocent said. "Why is it so hard to get a girl to swallow a load? Just take one for the team and do it. I mean, do you think every guy loves going down on a chick? Hell fucking no, but we do it. Am I right guys?"

"I think you're on your own on this one," The Hitman remarked.

"Oh c'mon! Really?" The Innocent said.

"Here's the real deal, honey," The Woman said. "No woman likes to suck dick. It's the world's greatest lie. They will tell you they do all day long because you like it, but no woman wakes up that day hoping for the chance to suck a dick."

"That's bullshit! There are plenty of girls who tell me they love it," The Serial Killer exclaimed, "usually because I'm forcing them at gunpoint, but still!"

"Fuck you, asshole!" The Woman picked up a bullet

from the Pile and threw it at him. The Serial Killer returned the favor with a well-placed projectile to her neck. "That's the closest you'll ever get to shooting me," The Woman smiled.

"Is this truly the course of action we're choosing to partake in?" The Pacifist asked. The Terrorist quickly struck him in the forehead with a bullet. Everyone around the table laughed.

"That's what happens when a pacifist gets mixed up in war," The Hitman chuckled.

"Oh, so you think you're getting out of here alive?" The Woman said. She picked up a bullet and threw it at The Hitman but missed.

"No, but I'll make sure I see your body being dragged out of here first," The Hitman said. He threw another bullet at The Woman, this one bouncing off the table and hitting her in her chest.

From out of nowhere, a bullet hit The Terrorist in the temple. The inmates looked at one another around the table. They could see that The Terrorist was angry, but The Pacifist was smiling. "Sorry, I couldn't help myself," The Pacifist laughed. "It looked like fun."

"I knew the whole 'pacifist' thing was just an angle to not get a bullet in the head," The Hitman said.

"Pacifism is only against acts of violence, and it's only violence if someone gets hurt intentionally. This is merely a skirmish," The Pacifist lectured. "And sometimes multiple skirmishes are needed." The Pacifist revealed a bullet palmed in his left hand and hurled it like a frantic pitcher, hitting The Serial Killer. The bullet bounced above ~~the~~ his eyebrow, ~~slicing the skin open and bleeding.~~ leaving his skin sliced open. Blood dripped down his face.

"Okay, now you're not a pacifist any longer because that really did hurt, you little bitch," said The Serial Killer.

"I...I'm really sorry. I didn't mean to hurt you," The Pacifist said, lowering his face in shame.

"Right, because bullets were never meant to hurt people?" The Serial Killer sneered.

"Looks like someone's getting their panties all in a bunch," The Woman commented.

"Fuck you, slut!" The Serial Killer shot back, blood trickling down his brow and onto his prison shirt.

"Hey, calm the fuck down everyone. It was an accident. You get more upset about someone throwing a bullet at you than you actually do someone shooting you," The Hitman reasoned. "Shut the fuck up and get over it." The Hitman ~~shot~~ glared at The Serial Killer, giving him an evil eye.

The buzzer echoed off the concrete walls. The Terrorist pointed the gun at The Hitman. "I'm sorry, my friend. It is out of respect, not hatred."

"I understand and respect your decision," The Hitman said proudly and waited for the gun to fire.

-Click-

The Innocent

The Hitman gave The Terrorist a nod signifying his respect for his decision. The Terrorist handed the gun over to The Innocent. The Pacifist started to talk as The Innocent placed the third bullet into the chamber. "It's still not too late to contemplate your life, you know?"

"What the fuck are you talking about?" The Innocent replied. "Our lives are over, why can't you get it through your skull?"

"Our lives are just beginning, can't you see that," The Pacifist said.

"Um...no, no we can't. Sorry but we don't speak 'new age'." The Innocent was annoyed by The Pacifist's comment.

"Or whack job," The Woman added.

"Listen, I don't care what your personal philosophy is *philosophies are* but if there is an afterlife, ~~I do believe that~~ this isn't the way to get to heaven," The Pacifist said.

"Why don't you get it, we're already fucked. There's nothing we can do to fix what we've already done," said The Woman.

"How many times are we going to run around in circles about this shit? We keep talking about the same fucking stuff again and again, but nothing is getting resolved," The Terrorist said. "We already know what we believe, and we're not going to make any progress on this shit, and that's it."

"Maybe so, but even if there's the slightest chance of an afterlife, isn't it worth it?" The Pacifist said. "Truth be told, no one knows what happens after you die, but isn't it better to believe in something, just in case?"

"Pascals Wager is a bullshit argument and you know it," The Hitman said. "You're judged by how good of a person you are, and the last time I checked, we're all fucked there. There's nothing we can do about that now." The room sat silent as his words sank in.

"Well if that's the case, we might as well spill what the worst thing we've ever done. You start," The Terrorist said pointing to The Serial Killer.

"There are books about the worst things I've ever done. I am not the most interesting person to start this," The Serial Killer said.

"What about the things no one knows about, the one's you actually feel bad about?" The Terrorist asked.

"You're right, I never felt bad about slicing up those sluts, but I did rape a girl once. Not any of the ones I killed, mind you, but this was before I started killing. I was in college and there was this woman, I think her name was Danielle. She was that kind of chick I always wanted but was just out of my league, you know what I'm sayin'? I was at a dorm party and she was there, drunk as fuck, and I wasn't. So I fucked her in the bathroom. I still can't forgive myself for that." The Woman was surprised that he gave an honest answer and didn't respond with his usual sarcastic rhetoric. The Innocent looked confused.

"Wait! Why would you feel bad about that? I mean, that's not a bad thing to do, is it? Hell, if I didn't do that, my sexual encounters would be half of what it is," The Innocent said.

"Yeah, it really is bad. It makes you a gigantic pile of shit, actually. You knowingly took advantage of women," The Serial Killer said.

"You killed them! I just showed them a good time, how is that even remotely bad? At least I never killed any of them," The Innocent said, shrugging his shoulders in confusion.

"Right, you only kill the ones you loved? Yup, you sure are standing on a moral high ground," The Serial Killer remarked.

"Fuck you, I didn't kill my family. I'm not like you," The Innocent said.

"Oh that's right, I forgot. You're innocent, right? No one believes that shit," The Serial Killer said. "Even if it were true, you're still guilty of being an asshole." The Innocent cocked back the hammer of the gun and stood up.

"You wanna die, cocksucking motherfucker? I don't care if I have to keep pulling the trigger until your head is gone.

I'll do it. I'll blast your face out of this room, you impotent prick," The Innocent shouted.

"Yup, that sure does sound like someone who's never killed before. Just fucking admit it, you killed your family. You can regret it all you want, but you're still a cock-bag."

A voice of one of the guards came through a speaker in the room reminding the prisoners that any more than one pull of the trigger in each round would result in a "disqualification" of the game.

"You really think I give a shit? I already know I'm dead!" The Innocent yelled at the speaker. "The only reason I even want out of here is to try and find the killer. I want to find the person who really should be in this room right now instead of me. Do you have any idea how hard it is when nobody believes you? When no one believes that you wouldn't kill the ones you love the most? Do you? Do you? You can all fuck yourselves. Just put me out of my fucking misery, I really couldn't care less. Maybe I'll do the same thing as The Preacher and just blow my brains out. Is that what you guys want? Is it? Is it? The only family I have left thinks I'm a murderer. Do you think any of my friends are going to let me crash at their place? I was a fucking hotel manager, for Christ's sake! Do you think I have some sort of hidden stash of money to live off? Give me one good reason not to just pull this fucking trigger on all of you right now! I'm as good as dead anyways," The Innocent said.

"Hope," The Pacifist said. "You still hope that you can get out of here and find the person who really murdered your family." The Innocent put the gun back down on the table, breathing heavily.

"You're right. I have to try for her, for them," The Innocent said. The buzzer went off. "You deserve this," The Innocent picked the gun up and aimed the gun at The Serial Killer. "And I'm sorry."

-Click-

The Pacifist

The Innocent, exasperated, banged his head against the table and handed the gun off to The Pacifist. The Pacifist clumsily placed the fourth bullet in the chamber. He gently and neatly placed the gun back on the table. "So my lady, what's the worst thing you've ever done?" The Pacifist asked with a smile, nodding towards The Woman.

"I guess that just depends on what the ranking is. What's worse than what?" The Woman asked. She pondered all the sins of her past, a finger over her lips.

"We've already established that rape is worse than murder for a serial killer, and we've come to the conclusion that rape is okay if you haven't killed anyone according to an innocent," The Terrorist said as a matter of fact. Both The Innocent and The Serial Killer gave The Terrorist the same look of disgust.

"Well fuck it! I guess I'll let you decide what's considered worse. The one situation that I can't forgive myself for happened when I was about twenty-one. I sucked my dealer's dick for coke. It was the only time I ever did that for hard drugs. I thought it would be better if I didn't have to pay for it," The Woman said. "Falling in love with a friend is another of my biggest regrets, but I'm sure you wouldn't rank that up there very high."

"Why is that such a big regret?" The Pacifist asked. "I mean, yeah it can turn out bad, but how much worse could it be than hurt feelings?"

"Murder, it ended in murder." The Woman shook her head in shame. "Another big regret that I have is when I was seventeen, I had an abortion. I told myself I did it because I couldn't tell my mother, but she wouldn't have cared anyway. I just wasn't ready to give up my youth. Not that it mattered, my future wasn't what I thought it would be," The Woman said lost in thought. She wondered about how her life could have turned out if she had made a different decision. Would she still have been forced to strip to make ends meet? Would she have sucked paid favors for coke? Would she be sitting in this room now? She didn't know, but she didn't like to ~~ponder~~ think of such questions for very long.

"If you could go back in time and change one of those experiences, which one would you change" The Pacifist asked.

"The abortion...not because I think it's wrong because I don't think it's wrong. It's a woman's right to choose, but I think if I had given birth to my child, my life would be very different. If I had not had the abortion, maybe the bad shit that's happened in my life wouldn't have happened, you know?" The Woman said. "What about you? What's the worst thing you've ever done?"

"The worst thing I've ever done is losing my temper. I

should have never lost my temper like I did. I should have had a higher degree of emotional intelligence to know it was only going to end badly. I betrayed who I am, and I think that is the worst thing one can do to themselves," The Pacifist said.

"Care to elaborate a little bit? You're being vague again," The Terrorist responded.

"I caught my wife cheating on me, and I overreacted, to put it lightly," The Pacifist confessed. "I told her I was going to kill her, and I felt like I had to follow through with my threat."

"I don't think 'peer pressure murder' would have gone over too well in courts, eh?" The Hitman said.

"No, I suppose not. It's hard for me to imagine that I'm even the same person as I was back then," The Pacifist said.

"Don't sweat it baldy. Women can make men think and do crazy shit that they normally wouldn't do," The Innocent remarked.

"I suppose, sometimes, that's a true statement, however it does not excuse my actions, what I did. Don't get me wrong, she wasn't innocent, Not by a long shot, but I should have just left. It wasn't something I needed to kill her over. Sure she betrayed me fucked me over bad, but she didn't deserve to die over it. I know better than anyone that you can't take back what you've done no matter how hard you try to make amends. There's no point on dwelling on the past though. That's why you must look forward to the future," The Pacifist said hanging his head in shame. Tears slipped down his face and ~~puddled~~ gathered on the table.

"Well, um, I guess I'll go next," The Terrorist volunteered.

"Where the hell are you going, bomb making convention?" The Serial Killer joked.

The Terrorist looked over at The Serial Killer. "You know what I mean, the worst thing I've ever done."

"Hold on, let me guess. You did Americans in for the off chance of getting seventy six virgins when you die?" The Innocent mocked.

"Seventy two, it's seventy two virgins in Houri," The Hitman corrected him.

"Oh, my bad. Seventy six virgins just sounds too ridiculous," The Innocent replied.

"Do you want to hear it, or do you want to keep on bickering about how many virgins I'm going to fuck when I die?" The Terrorist asked. The inmates quietened down, interested in what the Terrorist had to confess. The Serial Killer hoped to hear something more sinister than he could think of. "I participated in a group beating when I was in high school," The Terrorist confessed. "Me and my friends each took turns beating this kid with a baseball bat. He ~~had~~ snitched on one of our friends. We ended up sending him to the hospital. They said he had to get over 100 stitches. The kid was lucky to even be alive after we were done with him. The funny thing is, even though he knew who we all were, he never snitched on any of us for it." The Serial Killer was disappointed.

"What did he do?" The Woman asked. The Terrorist didn't respond, only raised his eyebrows. The Woman continued, "What did your friend do in the first place for this kid to snitch on him?"

"My friend was cheating on his girlfriend. Real high school type drama, I know, but they were serious. They were talking about getting married. When he told her that he had been cheating, there was no way he could get her back. It was over," The Terrorist said. "That destroyed him. After he graduated high school, he went into the military."

The Woman looked at him puzzled. "So he beat someone because he couldn't keep his dick in his pants? Yeah, that sounds like something guys would do."

The Serial Killer interrupted. "Look, I know you don't have a penis and therefore lack reason, honey bunny, but it's guy code that you just don't break. He snitched not because it was the right thing to do, but because he knew it would break them up. He wanted his friend's girl's ass for his own. You know, playing the ol' sympathetic friend card. Usually works when the girl is vulnerable."

"Exactly," The Terrorist agreed, giving The Serial Killer a deep nod.

"Guys are pathetic," The Woman said, rolling her eyes and crossing her arms ~~across~~ over her chest.

"It's not so much that men are pathetic, it's that women are too dumb to realize the tactic works," The Serial Killer mentioned. "We wouldn't waste our time if it didn't get us a nobber at least half of the time." The buzzer sounded, startling The Serial Killer. The Pacifist grabbed the gun off of the table and raised it into the air. He pulled the trigger, aiming at no one.

Russian Poker

-Click-

The Woman

The Pacifist passed the gun like a whiskey shot in a western movie across the table. The Woman chose a bullet from the pile on the table and pointed it at The Serial Killer. "You know what this is, prick?" she asked, "This is the bullet that's going to kill you. You're not getting off easy this time."

"If you flapped as much lip at the blow job factory where you were employed, you would easily have been a millionaire by now," The Serial Killer said. The Woman picked up the revolver and placed the fifth bullet into it a little too eagerly.

"Get your insults in while you can, fuckface. You know your time is up. You know deep down this is it. I. Am. Going. To. Kill. You," The Woman said tapping the tip of the gun on the metal table with each word.

The Serial Killer leaned back into his chair, putting his hands behind his head. "Then someone else is going to get the gun and is going to shoot you," he said. "Then someone else is going to kill them until only one of us is left in this hellhole. Then the guards will shoot you at point blank, piss on your body and throw confetti. How many times do I have to say that I already know I'm dead? There is no prize at the end of this. I'm just enjoying what little time I have left while I still have it. Hopefully I get a couple more rounds to call you a whore."

"Well I guess you're still staying true to what you believe, I'll at least give you credit for that," The Innocent said.

"Aww thanks, that means a lot to me coming from a guy who stuck to his guns and made sure every nigga was properly taken care of," The Serial Killer taunted.

"Fuck you! I had no problems with The Preacher. That gang banger had it coming though. I'm not even the one who killed him! I haven't killed anyone, remember?"

"Yeah, that's what you keep saying Mr. Holier Than Thou." The Serial Killer rolled his eyes.

"So since this will be the shot that kills you, anything you'd like to say? You better say it now while you still can," The Woman interrupted.

"Oh well, you know, I guess just the usual: you're a whore, when your ass is cashed in this room, you'll be sucking dick up in heaven since it's the only thing you were ever good at. And by looking at those lips of yours, you must be really good at it. No one will miss you except for one of your John's in a couple years, will think to himself, 'What ever happened to that one slut-bag that would suck my dick backwards for a hit of meth?'"

The Woman tightened her grip on the handle with each insult. "At least you'll be immortalized though: the best cum-guzzler in the great state of Texas. You'll probably get a statue. Generations to come will walk past the statue and turn to their mothers and ask, 'Hey Mommy, what made her so special?' And the mom will tell her child, 'That, little Jimmy, is the woman who swallowed so much semen in one month that all of her eggs got impregnated at the same time. She had to get so many abortions that month that she single handedly saved the economy,'" The Serial Killer laughed at his own handiwork. The anger rose to The Woman's face, turning her red.

The livid look in her eyes only egged The Serial Killer on more. "When aliens come and destroy us all, they will leave this statue fully intact and take it back to their planet because the sexual feats of a single human woman has out sucked and fucked their entire species."

R.L. Murphy

-Bang-

The Story of Tom Shades

center

"How many do I have to kill before I'm famous?"

Some people have it, some people don't. I've known for a long time that I have it. There are two types of people who kill. There are those who don't want to be caught, and then there are those who do. For me, it's all about the game. It's a game to see how many times I can get away with it before they catch on. I compare it to bowling: if you bowl the same way each time, you'll always bowl a perfect game. I'm going after strike (twenty-eight) tonight. *he only killed 13?!4?*

I'll admit, I do meet the essential criteria of the stereotypical serial killer. I was abused as a kid, both sexually and physically. When I was young, all I wanted was attention. I would take it from anywhere I could get it. Maybe attention isn't the right word I'm looking for. Infamy, that's it. I wanted to be infamous. I'd be lying if I told you I didn't get hard walking down the street hearing woman talking about being scared of leaving their homes at night because of me.

When the majority of people die, their family and friends are the only people who remember them. Once those people are dead and gone, it's as if that person never existed. I can't have that happen to me. I need to be remembered. I want to be remembered long after I'm dead. When I made the decision to never be forgotten, I knew I didn't want to be remembered for something good, I don't have it in me to be good. I would have to be immortalized for doing something nefarious. I needed to prepare for this if I wanted to be remembered for my misdeeds. I planned my legacy for a year before putting anything into action.

Every serial killer needs a gimmick or a trademark. What is the point in killing someone in the first place if they can't attribute the kill to you? The gimmick or trademark is that little something that shows that this killing was completely intentional. It's a middle finger to the law enforcement, which I love. Because of that, the media will always give you a nickname. Unfortunately you never get to choose it. I would imagine John Wayne Gacy probably never wanted to be remembered as the "creepy clown guy". That was his fault. Maybe if he had worked on a commercial boat he would have been called "The Shrimp Boat Killer". Lucky for me, "The Accountant Killer" doesn't have a ring to it.

I decided I wanted to tattoo my victims. That would be my undeniable trademark. It took me weeks to decide on what to tattoo and where. It needed to be something consistent and distinguishable just in case of copy cat killers. You know those amateurs, those unoriginal bastards who want only to ride on your coat tails while you are the one doing all the back breaking work. I decided on tattooing the acronym "KBT." I would place it on the ankle of my victims for "Killed By Tom".

For one, the authorities would believe it was my initials. Secondly, they would be searching for someone covered in tattoos and piercings, you know the kind. That isn't me. The only ink I have on me is a dumb skull that I got when I was eighteen. This was my way of thwarting the police. Nothing brings me more joy than when I hear that they have some poor tattoo artist cocksucker in custody. It always makes me giddy.

Most people don't realize they actually are capable of killing someone. When they do realize that they can kill, they pick the wrong people. They choose to murder the assholes making them miserable. That's a sure fire way to get yourself propped up on a cold, steel gurney, and get injected with a big ol' shot of potassium chloride in front of a live studio audience. Don't kill people you know, and don't kill them in a way that will lead them to you.

How I kill has become a ritual for me. I always take the same precautions each time. I always wear black clothing. I always wear the same leather gloves. I always make sure the vehicle is parked outside of the range of any security cameras. And I always know where the security cameras are. I always make the kill inside the car. It doesn't matter how hard my dick gets, I never fuck the victim. And as always, I dump the victim in the same location, although I am careful to choose a different area within that location each time, as they set up patrols and cameras.

You never want to be seen with the woman you are going to kill. Once you are inside the bar, sit in a booth at the back and look for where the security cameras are. When the cops become frustrated with the case, they will resort to watching security tapes for hours on end. Let other guys buy her drinks, and then tell them to piss off. Follow behind her fifteen seconds after she leaves. Fifteen seconds is just long enough to easily track her down, but not long enough for her to get into her car while in her inebriated state. Cops never watch the videos that long after they leave. Strike up a conversation, convincing her that you should drive her home since she's obviously intoxicated. Resist the urge to fondle her, and reject any advances she makes. This will happen. You don't need any DNA floating around inside her bloated body when it surfaces. Dump her body in the same area as your other victims. You want the body to be found. How else can they admire your perfect strikes?

I'm in a rundown dive bar called Joe's Place in a rundown town a few miles away from my rundown home. This is the same place where I found my third victim. There is a bank across the street from the bar so I make sure to park my Camry out of sight from cameras around the building. Walking into Joe's Place, the first thing I notice is how someone tried to decorate by trying to make a re-creation of the Alamo on what looks like a fifty dollar budget. I usually know who ~~I'm going to~~ the lucky girl *is*

~~pick~~ immediately upon entering an establishment. Tonight, it's different. Tonight, I have choices. Tonight, there are two clear candidates.

My first candidate is dancing on a table. She's a redhead, probably in her early thirties, and it's not hard to tell this girl has a past. It's not hard to admire this chick. You can tell her past doesn't hold her back. She has shot down every guy that has hit on her, but it doesn't deter them in the least. She's one of those girls that you can't help but be mesmerized by even though she's not that physically attractive. There's something deep inside your brain that insists you need her. In the Middle Ages, she would have been deemed a succubus. In today's age, she's a D-cup destroyer of men.

The other candidate is a mousy looking brunette who appears to be in her late twenties. I watch as she knocks back Jack and cokes, one right after another, all night long. The few men that do approach her, she is able to defend off like the battle of the bulge. She looks recently divorced. I imagine her husband probably left her for his lover and ever since, she has been hitting the bars, justifying to herself that all men are pigs.

The redhead won't give me trouble. I know I can talk her into going home with me without any problems. The only problem I see with her is the other guys. They'll be lined up just to follow her out the door, and I don't need to be seen. They'll follow her out of the place like she was the pied piper of penis.

The mousy brunette will just need some convincing...no worries.

11:30

After five or so Jack and cokes, the mousy brunette picks up her purse, searching in its depths for her keys. This is my cue. I throw thirty dollars on the table. I never use credit or debit cards to pay for my tab. The detectives will cross check names across databases, and I don't need mine showing up. There's nothing better than the feeling of stepping out of a hot ass, stuffy bar into a cold night. It's always so refreshing, and it sets just the right mood for tonight's events. She fumbles with her keys in the door of her car, just like every horror movie I've ever fantasized about.

"Hey there. It looks as though you may have had one too many to drink," I say as I approach her. "Do you need a ride?"

"I don't even know you," she replies in a wispy, high pitched voice. "Like I'm just going to get into a car with you. I'm not getting raped tonight, so just fuck off!"

"Listen Sweetheart, I just don't want my epitaph to say 'here lies the dude who was killed by a drunk driver. Even though she was offered a safe ride home, she walked away'." I can see that she's listening to me, even if she's drunk as fuck. I continue. "No offense but the guys aren't falling over you, and I can see why." I look her up and down, helping her notice what a sloppy mess she is. "I don't want you hurting anyone else out there tonight. If you manage to kill some hot bitch who wants to blow me, I don't think I'll be able to forgive you."

"Very funny," she slurs out. "But maybe you're right. You can drop me off at my place, but if you try anything..."

"Yeah, yeah, I know," I cut her off. "Mace me, rip my balls off, then make me dance the electric slide until the apocalypse, I get it."

"Just because you think you're funny doesn't mean I'm going to give you a break from dancing." She smiles. I thought I'd have to try a little harder with her but this is good. I know I have her. The fish in the lake will be nibbling at her toes in no time!

She is cautious as she walks behind me to my car. I get in the car and reach over the passenger seat to unlock her door. She opens the door and gets in.

"Nice bumper sticker," she says.

"Which one? The 'There's a body in the trunk' or the 'Learn Spanish! Jesus is coming'?" I ask.

"The Jesus one."

"It might help if you tell me where you live," I say as I start the car.

"Just drop me off on the corner of Third and Main."

"Hey, isn't that where the Chinese place is?"

"That's actually why I moved there. When I was a little

girl, I thought I would be happy forever if I lived next to a Chinese restaurant...I was so wrong."

"I said the same thing in college, but about strip clubs...but I was right!"

"Classy," she remarks as she lights a cigarette. Virginia Slims...figures.

"No smoking, hun. Sorry but I have asthma." I am not willing to take the chance from her cigarette. Her saliva from the damn cancer stick she's sucking on is enough DNA to lay me on that cold, steel gurney. "Just throw it out the window," I tell her. "I'm not a cop, I'm not going to write you a ticket." She rolls down the window and throws her half smoked cigarette out of the car. I notice her obedience to directions. This is good.

"I don't usually take this way home. Isn't it quicker to just go through downtown?" she asks, her voice getting a bit quivery. She is nervous. I don't need her to bail out on me now, especially in a public place.

"I know, but even though I had one drink two hours ago, with all the cops around, they'll still hit me with a DUI down at county." It's hard having a quick mind all the time.

"Yeah probably. It happened to me a few years ago," she replies. We're three blocks away from the spot. Just like bowling, do it the same way every time. Park in the alley, stab her in the neck, tattoo her after she stops moving, toss the body in the trunk, drive to the lake, and last but not least, dump the corpse. Do it the same way every time. My grip on the steering wheel tightens as we get closer to the spot. I can feel the adrenaline start to course through my body. I start grinding my teeth. I do this every time right before the kill. I've never been able to figure out why.

"I think my tire is losing air. Mind if I pull over and check the air pressure?" I ask.

"I guess not. Just be quick about it," she says seeming a little concerned again.

"It doesn't matter where you live, there will always be assholes throwing nails in the road. Who the fuck does that?" I pull into the alley. This is the spot. "I guess this will have to do." I take the keys out of the ignition, step out of the car and into the alley. I walk to the back of the car, pop open the trunk and take out the knife and tattoo gun. Everything is all set to go. Deep breath. Okay, just open her door and stab her in the neck. I calmly walk to the passenger side. I lift up on the handle. It doesn't open like it's supposed to. The dumb bitch locked it. I cup my face over the window, looking inside and playing it cool.

"What's going on? C'mon, it's cold out here. Jokes over, the tire is fine." Oh shit, she opened the glove box. She must have thought I had a fucking tire gauge in the glove box.

"What's this?" she mouthed from inside the car. She holds up a photo of a woman's leg, letters "KBT" tattooed in my handwriting across it. She's on her cell phone. Fuck! Fuck! She can't find her goddamn car keys in her fucking mess of a purse but she can certainly find her goddamn cell phone! This is it, I gotta get to her quick. I take the back end of the knife and shatter the passenger side window.

"Come here, you little whore." I slip up. What the fuck am I doing? Don't talk, she's on the fucking phone. I don't need a recording of my voice floating around. I don't hesitate. I stab her in her clavicle, the knife scraping against the bone. I pull the blade out and jam it into her throat until I feel it slice straight through to the headrest. I leave it in. Pulling it out will mean I'll be cleaning up her mess for days and I can't have that. It'll take a few minutes for her lungs to fill up with blood. In the meantime, I gotta get the fuck out of here. I grab the cell phone out of her hand and launch it into the darkness of the alley.

"Look, you're already dead. No one is coming to save you from this," I say to her. Blood is gurgling down her neck. "If I pull this knife out, you're gonna die in a matter of seconds. Pray, confess, do whatever you have to do because you're not getting out of this alive." Even though I don't give a shit about her, I can't help but feel a little sympathetic about her situation. I pull out of the alley and drive towards the lake. I don't know what she told the fucking cops but I can't allow that to divert me from the plan now. Stay the course, I tell myself. Stick to the fucking rules. She's silent but still alive. The cold wind rushing in from the broken passenger side window is probably keeping her awake and conscious. I throw her cell phone out the broken window.

"I guess you figured it out by now. I'm the one and only Prairie Dog Killer," I confess to her. I can only imagine what the wind feels like against the ~~wound~~ gash in her throat. She keeps staring forward, acting like I don't exist. "You are tonight's victim but you fucked that all up. Since it doesn't matter what you know, I'll tell you what the media hasn't figured out. 'KBT' aren't my initials. It stands for 'Killed by ~~Ted~~ Tom'. It was my initials I would use in arcade games whenever I beat someone's high score...killed by ~~Ted.~~ Tom I'm just a regular guy, hun. I work as an accountant. I just have an interesting hobby." She was struggling to say something to me. I watched as her mouth moved up and down but no voice could be heard. "Don't bother to try talking about yourself. I'll learn your story when your picture shows up on the front page of the newspaper tomorrow or the next day. The only victim I felt bad about killing was the doctor...I had no idea who she was until I saw her on the news. I mean, she was just a podiatrist but still, ya know?"

Tears stream down her cheeks. I guess talking about seeing her picture on the news got to her, made this whole event real to her. "We're almost there. Just hang on a bit longer." I feel this overwhelming sharp pain in my thigh. "Ah, fuck!" I yell. I look down to see the knife I used on her sticking out of my leg. She's pulled out the knife from her neck and stabbed me with it. That little bitch! I can't move it. The knife went all the way through my thigh and into the driver's seat. I look over at her. The blood from her neck is spurting all over the windshield. I must have tagged her jugular vein whenever I stabbed her. She stares at me with her dark brown eyes and starts smiling. The muscles in her neck pull back making the gash in her neck widen. Blood squirts out of the gash like an overflowing juice box.

As her last act of defiance, she grabs the steering wheel, pulling it violently to the right and straight into a guard rail. All I can see is the one headlight reflecting off of the lake, the same lake that I got my nickname from. She tries to speak again but all I can hear is blood gurgling in her throat. I can almost understand what she is trying to say.

"I kill you now," I hear through the gurgling. "I kill the killer."

One year later

The stupid bitch was wrong. I lived and she died two minutes later in the car, her blood all over me. The fucking detective on her case was an idiot. It took him a week to figure out who I was. I left the tattoo gun in the car for Christ's sake! They were going to chock it up to attempted rape and manslaughter. The geniuses finally put the pieces together after they realized the car was left next to my dumping grounds. I'm being sentenced right now but what's the fucking point? They know what I did, and I'm getting death. "Is there anything you'd like to say to the families of the victims and all those your unforgivable actions caused harm to?" The obese, balding judge asked, his voice cold and harsh.

I smiled at the audience before me and said, "Yes I would. I made a mistake, and I want to ask for forgiveness for that. I should have chosen the redhead."

The Body of Tom Shades

The bullet blasted out of the gun and into the forehead of Tom Shades. His head jerked back, ~~hitting and~~ left to dangle over the back of the chair. His Adam's apple protruded out of his neck. The blood *slowly leaked* from the bullet hole left his forehead ~~and~~ ~~hit the floor in a slow leak~~ *beneath him. dripping down the neck onto the floor*. ~~It was heard by all the inmates in the room~~. The Woman was relieved*,* ~~and~~ *and* satisfied by the death of The Serial Killer. "How does it feel to be killed by a whore? No jokes now, huh, you stupid bastard! Can't call anyone names now*,* you stupid piece of shit, can ya?" The Woman ~~spit~~ *spat* at Tom's body*,* *instead* but it hit the edge of the table. She didn't notice the guards as they came into the room ~~as she spat~~.

"See Jimmy, I told you she spits. You owe me a drink," The Tall Guard laughed as he nudged The Short Guard in the ribs.

The Woman leaned over to The Short Guard and whispered in his ear, "If you let me go, I'll suck you off." The Short Guard grinned. He was obviously turned on by her advances, but he shook his head.

"Sorry babe, you're more important to me in this room," The Short Guard whispers back into her ear. "I'm sorry.." The Short Guard took the gun from the hands of The Woman and emptied it of the four remaining bullets. He placed them back ~~onto~~ *into the pile* the table while The Tall Guard dragged Tom's body out of the room.

The Hitman

The Hitman placed a single bullet into the chamber of the gun and locked it shut. "So it looks like this is the halfway point," he remarked. "Five of us found steel in our faces, five of us haven't. I wish it could end here and we could all call it a day...but as you all know, we can't. If we're lucky, one of us gets out, but I think we're to the point where we can talk about it."

"I don't think any of us want to die. If we did, we would have done so by now," The Terrorist said.

"Of course we all want out of here, but do you think you really deserve it? Do you think you should be the one who leaves this room alive?" The Hitman asked.

"Umm, yeah, I think I'd be pretty okay with that," The Innocent said.

"You should know better. No amount of politicking is going to not make us want to live. Valiant effort however, but no dice," The Pacifist said.

"It's funny you should say that," The Hitman remarked. "You were the one I was talking about. Wouldn't it be really nice to ensure we wouldn't be in danger this round? If we kill him, it won't be one of us, and we know he won't shoot us."

"I'm game," The Terrorist said.
"I'm in too," The Innocent agreed.

"I don't think that's right. The man is sitting right here

in front of you! How can you just say that in his face? You're talking about agreeing to kill the man right in front of him," The Woman said.

"You didn't seem to mind when it was you doing the killing," The Terrorist said, confronting her.

"Fuck you! He deserved it and you know it," The Woman replied, blowing her hair out of her face.

"It's only different because you're not the one with the gun," The Hitman said. "Well then, I guess we don't agree. Let's continue with our little game, you know, 'the worst thing I've ever done' thing. We never fully went around the table. I guess it's my turn.

"The worst thing I've ever done, is the only thing I've ever regretted. I was eighteen, and just got into the business. I was hired to set up this kid named Kenny. He owed his bookie a lot of money and needed some motivation to pay up. I had to get close to Kenny for him to trust me. I wasn't the hitman, I just had to get him to go to the hit spot. I went to the bar Kenny regularly went to, and acted like I accidentally bumped into him. I apologized and bought him a drink. I know that no matter where I go people want to talk to me because of how I look. Kenny wasn't an exception."

The Hitman shifted slightly and resumed his story. "For the next two months we became really close friends. We went bowling, smoked pot, watched movies together. Kenny really became a good friend of mine. The day of the hit came at the three month mark. I called Kenny and told him there was a new Thai restaurant I wanted to try. I picked him up and drove into town. On the way there, we talked about his life and what he wanted to do with the rest of it. He didn't know he didn't have one. He told me he wanted to get his act together, and follow his dreams of being a chef. We pulled into the parking lot where I was supposed to bring him for the hit. The hired hitman tapped on my window with his gun. I lowered his window. Kenny looked towards him, then at me. I saw that Kenny didn't care that he knew he was about to die, he cared that I betrayed him. He cared about what we had that wasn't real. The hitman leaned over me and shot him. My face was the last thing Kenny saw. The last thing he felt was betrayal. That's a terrible thing to take from someone. That's the worst thing I've ever done..." The Hitman's voice trailed off as he tried to finish his story. He looked up and noticed The Woman had a tear rolling down her face.

"I...I...I know just what you mean," The Woman said, fresh tears flowing from her eyes. "I've felt that before. There's nothing you can do about it now."

"Except deal with the consequences of it. The sooner you accept your actions for what they are, the sooner your spirit will be free," The Pacifist said.

"More of this spiritual bullshit?" The Innocent

189

remarked. He began to bang his head against the steel table.

The Hitman spoke up. "I think he's right. I don't think we can hold onto things like that. It really doesn't do any good. Why hold onto something that you can never change? The only reason I can come up with, is to not make the same mistake again in the future."

"Do you think you're in danger of making the same mistake again?" The Terrorist asked.

"No, of course not. To be fair though, I don't think I'll have the opportunity given our present situation."

"I don't know about that. We have a twenty five percent chance of getting out of here," The Terrorist said. The Woman looked at The Terrorist puzzled.

"You're not doing the math wrong. He's insinuating that I'm not a threat and wouldn't count. I don't like thinking that way, but I guess he's not incorrect," The Pacifist replied.

"I still don't buy your bullshit for one second," The Hitman remarked. "You're just waiting for the moment to pull off your sheep's clothing. I don't think you're less dangerous than anyone else in this room. In fact, I believe you to be more so. You have them fooled."

"Really? If he was going to do that, wouldn't he have done so by now? He's been shot at enough times for it not to make sense," The Woman said.

"I think it's just the opposite. The more we shoot at

him, the safer he feels. And the safer he feels, the less of a threat we think he is," The Hitman replied. "However I still don't think you're the biggest threat in this room. When we are all convinced you're a lying sack of shit, we're all going to make sure you don't leave this room alive. Your strategy is hoping you live long enough so the odds are in your favor. Isn't that right?"

"I'm simply a man of peace. I know I'm going to die in here, and unlike you, I've come to terms with that. I came to grips with my own mortality when I was sitting on death row. I deserve to die. I'm not denying that. Getting another chance at life is only merely grace, nothing more."

The buzzer rang. The Pacifist closed his eyes. The Hitman aimed the barrel of the gun at The Terrorist. "I guess we're going to keep shooting at each other until one of us is gone?" The Hitman remarked. The Terrorist gave him a nod of respect. The Hitman pulled the trigger.

-Click-

The Terrorist

The Hitman returned a nod of respect to The Terrorist, slinging the gun across the table towards him. The Terrorist caught it and placed the second bullet into the chamber, snapping it shut. He laid it on the table. "So what are you going to do if you get out?" The Terrorist asked. "First thing out of the gate, you got five hundred dollars in your pocket, where do you go?"

"I would probably seek out a Buddhist monastery and live a life of peace for the rest of my life," The Pacifist said.

"Well first off, to get out of here alive, you'd have to kill at least one person. That would make you not such a peaceful person now, wouldn't it? Secondly, where the hell are you going to find a fucking Buddhist monastery in this country?" The Innocent asked.

"You would be surprised what exists in this country. Yes, they have monastery's that you live in. You don't have to worry about going to an office to work, paying rent, or what celebrities are up to. You just...live."

"Why the fuck would you want to do that? What's the point?"

"Enlightenment and a meaningful life. Besides, who else is going to take us in? We're murderers, we're not heroes. What else could we want but to help others in a small community and solve the mysteries of the universe?"

"Right, because Buddhists have been around for how long, and don't accept any of their 'truths'?" The Hitman said.

"The truth doesn't matter. Anyone who tries to get you to believe things that cannot be proven is probably trying to get into your wallet, nothing more. However, self truths only have to be true to you."

"So as long as you believe it, it becomes true?" The Woman asked, trying to piece together the message The Pacifist was trying to convey.

"Yes, more or less that's what I mean," The Pacifist said as he gave The Woman a nod of greater understanding.

"You know, I didn't notice it before but this room has an echo to it. I guess it's just because it's quieter in here now," The Woman remarked.

"Or you just couldn't hear it over his ramblings," The Terrorist said, as he pointed to The Serial Killer's empty chair. The five remaining inmates sat silently, waiting for something to happen. The buzzer went off.

"I guess we know this routine by now, don't we friend?" The Terrorist asked.

"I suppose we do, friend," The Hitman said snarling his upper lip.

"Just so you know, I don't believe this is your time," The Terrorist confessed.

"Neither did the people I killed right before I pulled the trigger. No one knows when they're going to die, even when they are staring down the barrel of a gun."

-Click-

The Innocent

The Terrorist grabbed the gun by the barrel and extended the handle to The Innocent. He took it and placed the third bullet in the gun, finally feeling comfortable with handling it. No one noticed anything about it. He was proud of himself. There was an appeal to owning a gun. It gave some sort of power The Innocent didn't have in his day to day life. He always wanted to own a gun but was too afraid to have one in his home. He didn't want the responsibility of having to worry about it. He knew he drank too much, and that his wife had enough anger in her to let a bullet loose into him after he got rough with her. The truth was he was afraid he felt so guilty for everything he had done wrong in his life that he would end up taking his own life. He never wanted to kill anyone, even if they did deserved it.

It occurred to The Innocent that he might have to kill someone in the next few minutes. He realized that every time the gun was placed into his hands before, he was allowing his emotions to get the best of him. He was acting out of irrational thought. This time he was calm. The Innocent didn't want to kill anyone, let alone someone around this table with him now. He felt an oddly close bond with the remaining inmates, did they he wondered to himself. they felt the same. He had pulled the trigger on several people but the only one that drew the gun on him was The Gangster. It had been over an hour since The Gangster death. Maybe his fellow inmates recognized that he was the only innocent person among them and that he deserved to live more than they did.

"So, uhh, what kind of sports are you guys into?" The Innocent asked, trying his best not to get into a serious discussion. Talking sports in Texas was about as safe a conversation as you can have in this world. "I mean, the Cowboys look pretty good this year. Am I right?"

"I was never much of a football guy. I was always more into hockey," The Hitman said.

"Get the fuck out of here with that shit! Really, you're into Canadian guys without teeth skating around ice?"

"I guess I can relate," The Hitman said, grinning his toothless smile. "Better than guys in padding from head to toe tackling each other on the soft grass on a Fall afternoon."

"So I've always wondered something about hockey: How do they not cut each other all the time? You would think it would happen a lot," The Woman asked. She had wondered for years but had never had the chance to ask.

"It doesn't happen often but a couple years back, a goalie had his neck slit. That's why hockey is great. He just held his neck as he was skating to the side lines," The Hitman said, covering his neck with his long, thin fingers.

"Oh wow, really? You would think I would have heard something about that."

"Hockey never makes the headlines. What about you?" The Hitman asked, nodding at The Terrorist.

"I only follow college basketball. It's the only sport worth watching. Go Buckeyes," The Terrorist said solemnly.

"I could never get into college basketball. There's just something about grown men arguing over which group of teenage boys is better than the rest of the teenage boys that doesn't appeal to me," The Pacifist said.

"Well, what are you into? What great and manly sport are you into?" The Terrorist asked the Pacifist.

"The only time I ever get into any athletic competition is The Olympics or World Cup."

"You're not making a good case for your sexual preference," The Innocent remarked.

"I just think there's something a bit more eloquent about athletes using their natural talents. They do it not for money, but to prove their country is the best," The Pacifist said, crossing his arms. "Plus, I don't have time to follow sports full time. Once every four years is all I think I can handle."

"What the hell have you been busy with since you've been in here?" The Woman asked.

"To be honest, being sentenced to death was liberating for me. The moment someone tells you when you're going to die, it sort of lifts a lot of the pressure off of you. More important, it tells you how much time you have left to do everything you want to do in your life. At that moment, sports, fashion, reality TV, even movies cease to matter. It turns into a game of how much knowledge can I put into my brain before it gets turned off?"

"So, what then," The Hitman replied, interested in what the Pacifist had to say. "You learn all you can just to have it ripped away from you in an instant? Why not have a good time while still you can? You can't regret having as much fun as you can when it's all over."

It's about learning as much as you can. When you allow Life to teach you, you learn how to be a better person so you can make the best choices when confronted with important decisions."

"None of that matters when there's a gun pointed in your face. You don't get choices when that happens."

"Then it is the person holding the gun that is making the uninformed choice, not me."

The buzzer sounded, scaring The Woman again. This scared The Innocent too. He knew by just pulling the trigger, he could end someone's life. He hoped that when he pulled the trigger that the gun wouldn't go off. He wanted to stay innocent. He picked the gun up off the table and pointed it at The Woman. "Please no! Don't do it! Please don't!" The Woman said, tears streaming down her face. He could feel her heart drop. "I don't want to die like this! Please!" She clenched her eyes tightly, feeling like a four year old getting ready for a shot at the doctor's office. She was sobbing heavily. Her entire face was wet with tears. "Please don't."

"I'm sorry. I'm no better than anyone else."

R.L. Murphy

-Bang-

The Story of Sandra "Candy" Collins

"How many must I kill before I'm beautiful?"

My alarm didn't go off! Shit! Shit! Shit! I look at the clock. It's 6:45 P.M. I have to be there in fifteen minutes! I make the decision to leave in my pajamas since I left my outfit at work.

I turn over to see who's lying beside me in between my eight hundred thread count Egyptian cotton sheets. I don't remember last night very well, but I'm pretty sure it's someone new.

He stirs under the sheets, placing his hand on my shoulder. His hand is soft, warm, and comforting. He's probably an emo-artsy kind of guy. I roll over. Instead of a faux-hawk and bad tattoos, I see the bright blue eyes and dull red hair of a woman. She smiles at me with a sleepy tenderness. There are cigarette stains on her teeth.

"Good Morning," she says.

"Yeah, I guess so. It's almost seven," I reply. "You need to get up. I have to leave in a few minutes."

"Oh c'mon, don't you want to go again?" She says with her slight southern drawl.

"To be honest, I don't remember and I think I'm good." She didn't care for my response.

"Can't you just leave your key for me? I don't want to

get up yet," she whines. She rolls back over, hugging my pillow. She has a butterfly tattoo on her back, so at least I got the bad tattoo part right.

"Only if you don't mind me calling the cops. Get the fuck out!"

"Okay jeez. You don't need to be such a bitch about it." She rolls her eyes.

"Yeah well, if I'm a bitch, so be it," I say. I watch as she gets out of my bed and I almost regret it. As the blankets slip off her body, I realize how beautiful she is despite her teeth and her God awful accent. She's one of those girls God made for the sole purpose of destroying the hopes and dreams of men...and apparently women too.

"What time do you hit stage tomorrow?" She asks, putting her tacky glass dolphin earrings back on. I wonder what made her think wearing porpoises in her ears was cute?

"Seven, same as always," I reply.

"I guess I'll see you then, right? I go in at five," she says. Fuck. I didn't realize that she's the new girl. Well this doesn't make things completely awkward or anything. At least she's getting out of here.

"I never got your name," I mention to her. A while ago, I promised myself I'd always know the name of everyone I slept with.

"Do you want my name or my 'name'?" She asks.

"It doesn't really matter. Stage name, real name, I just need something to call you."

"Just call me Mag, everyone else does," she says, stepping towards the door.

"Okay Mag, I'll see you tomorrow." Finally, she leaves. I step into my shoes and head out the door. It didn't hit me until I stepped outside but I'm still hungover from last night's party. The sun is still out and I can feel every ray beating against my head. That's Texas in July for you. At least I don't have to check the weather report. It's too late for me now to lock up my trailer, not that I have anything worth stealing. Who would want to steal cum stained sheets?

I unlock the passenger side door of my brown '93 Accord and get in. The driver side door broke after the last "incident". I climb over the center console and into the driver seat. I slide the key into the ignition, listening to the engine as it turns and starts up after ten or so seconds. Not a bad little car for a guy I blew a year ago. I really don't know which is worse, that a guy would offer to make a trade like that, or that I actually took him up on his offer. I guess it means that no matter how many rights women fight for, we will still need men in our lives. Or maybe, I guess it could mean that women will always have the means to pull one over on a man. I fear the day when men realize money is more important than sex. Until then, I still have a job.

Tonight is going to be one of those long nights, I can feel it. I pull in behind the fine establishment I work at, known as the Pink Triangle. Nothing says naked classy ladies like bad punch line to elementary school jokes. I reach for the keys to turn off the car when I realize the time on the dashboard. It's already 7:25, but it's fifteen minutes fast. Tony is going to give me shit about being late. That fat fuck thinks he owns me. No one owns me. I open the back door and smell Tony's rancid breath before I even see him.

"Where the fuck have you been?" Tony confronts me.

"I'm not giving you any bullshit excuses today, Tony," I say. "Get off my back. I need to get ready, I'll be on in a few minutes."

"You don't get to tell me what the fuck you're doing while you're on the clock, that's my fucking job!" He says, raising his voice at me. He sounds like a jazz singer with a mouth full of bourbon.

"Look, I'm sorry, Tony. It won't happen again, okay?" I try my best to sound as sorry as I can. Even if it was shitty, I still needed this job. "I'm just going through some stuff right now, you know, like womanly stuff." The first day on the job, Sarah told me that talking about your period makes Tony drop any conversation he may be having with you. Good trick to know.

"Alright whatever, just get your ass ready, You've already wasted enough time," Tony says as he shuffles into his office. I could see Tony's back hairs poking through his thin white shirt. I can smell the tramp spray as I open the door to the dressing room. I'm not sure why cherry body spray is the scent of every stripper in the world, but it certainly is true.

"Hey girl, where have you been?" I hear a familiar voice say. "We're supposed to dance together tonight. I didn't know if you wanted to be the cowgirl or the cop. I know you look really good in the cop outfit so I thought I would leave that one for you." It's Abigail, my only real friend. I don't know how some people can stay upbeat all the time, but she does it. It's something that I envy about her.

"Thanks Abby. You're the sweetest," I say, muffling as I dress up into the half-shirt that constitutes as a police uniform.

"I saw you leave with Mag last night," Abigail mentions.

"Yeah I guess I did. I don't even remember anything that happened. I don't know if being drunk made her any less abrasive or not," I say to Abby while adjusting my hat slightly to the right. I was trying my best to keep my pony tail tucked inside of it.

"Nopers. Mag's just as big of a meanie regardless of her state of intoxication," Abigail says with a wink. That girl is just too damned innocent and cute for her own good, but I never want her to change. The world hasn't corrupted her yet and I would like it to stay that way. That's probably why she's such a big draw around here. Guys like to think the women they fuck are innocent but they certainly don't want girls to act like that while we sucking them off.

"Okay, I'm almost ready. I just need a little motivation, and then I'll be ready to go." I pull out a small bag of cocaine from my drawer and snort a line.

"I wish you wouldn't do that. You know it's a terrible thing you are doing to your body," Abigail says, concerned over my well being. She starts biting her lower lip as if she was nervous to tell me.

"I know, I know, but I can't take your advice seriously while you're dressed like Calamity Jane. Are you ready Abby?" I ask.

"You know I prefer Abigail but yeah, let's go do this," Abby says. We walk together to the stage entrance. I was bumped down to Stage B for being late. It is closer to the bathroom, where the scumbags sit. They don't care for the rules very much. I can hear the song ending. The DJ is about ready to announce Abby and I, and hit my song. I still can't believe I got a pretty well-known band to record a song just for me to dance to. I could hear the echo of the voice.

"Ladies and gentleman, coming to the stage, the sweetest girl in the old Wild West, and the sexiest speeding ticket you'll ever get. Abigail and Candy!"

I step through the curtain as the lyrics "Don't you want my candy baby?" boomed over the speakers. The crowd cheers as the song continues. "Won't you give it one more lick?" The crowd always looks exactly the same when you're on stage, a bunch of old men, married assholes cheating on their wives, and college kids who think they've got enough "game" to score a stripper but never do.

I strut to the edge of the stage and pull a fake gun out of the holster around my hip. I stick my tongue against the plastic barrel, and slide it to the tip while making eye contact with the skinny college kid in the front row. His eyes are so wide you'd think he had found the fountain of youth. I wrap my full lips around the tip of the gun and then slowly pull it away from my face, then re-holster the fake weaponry.

I turn around, bending over in my skin tight blue daisy dukes. I reach my right hand around and slowly slide a finger along my ass. I arch my back and throw my hat towards the curtain. My blond hair hits me just below my shoulders. I can feel the hearts of several men dropping in the crowded club. I lean back as several patrons throw money on the stage. I bite my lower lip and unbutton the top three buttons of my shirt. My black bra hardly covers my nipples.

I drop to my hands and knees while my breasts hang barely above the floor. I crawl towards the left side of the stage, moving my hips to the beat of the music while making sure I do not pay too much attention to one side. I sit up with my legs spread wide in front of the bills thrown on stage. I pretend to touch myself over my daisy dukes as if this is how we actually do it. I take my fingers out of my panties and pretend to smell it.

A twenty dollar bill lands between my manicured toes. I bend over like I am taking a fitness test from middle school to see how far I can reach and grab the money. I grab it with my right hand and shove it into my pants, keeping it there, and pantomiming fondling myself with the dirty money. In a way, that's what this job is all about...money turns me on like ~~no~~ nothing else ~~other person~~ can.

A bill hits me in my nose, startling me. I stare at the man who threw it. It makes me so angry, I could spit nails. He's a man in his mid-fifties, wearing sweat pants that are pulled up over his enormous, pot belly stomach with his polo shirt tucked in. Gross! His mustache is graying from the middle and slowly creeping out. I guess he didn't get the memo that you don't wear polo shirts with sweat pants, The fat fuck never got one about facial hair being more than one color isn't a good thing either. I pick up the bill from the stage floor and un/crumple it...What the fuck? It's a fucking single? Who does this shithead think I am? I crumple it back up, spit on it, and throw it back in his face. Serves the motherfucker right! "I'm not a fucking whore!" I shout at him over the deafening music. He plucks the crumpled dollar bill from his emotionless face.

I go back to dancing as he casually walks out, looking

like he got bored. I pull my pants down teasingly, making sure the holstered plastic gun doesn't chip my cute toe nails. I undo the last two buttons from my shirt and take it off, still dancing to the music. Money is thrown at me like beer bottles slung at a bad heavy metal concert. I pick up the money in the usual manner, allowing it to slide across my tongue and then biting it. I cram it into my panties, or let the client shove it down between my breasts when I push them together. My favorite is having my male clientele stick their money into the back of my g-string. You're guaranteed to get at least a twenty each time.

I take off my bra forgetting about the twenty the drunken marine has placed there. It's hard for women with real breasts to convince the clientele that they're all natural when they look this damn good. Both of my nipples are hard. Not from being turned on, but from the line of coke I snorted a moment ago. I dance out the rest of the song, the lights dimming down to where I can see them but they can't see me.

I scoop up the remaining cash and grab my clothing, exiting backstage through the curtain. Abigail is holding her cowboy hat and chaps just as I walk through. Typical Abigail, she's making sure she doesn't drop anything. For a twenty year old, she really has herself together. She always gives her all in every dance. I find that I am really attracted to Abigail. I don't know how to express to her my feelings. I mean, we've kissed and fooled around before, but I would like something deeper with her. When I'm home by myself, I often wish I could be with her. Despite the happenings of this morning, I don't really consider myself a lesbian, I just don't like men much.

I know I can never be with her. She's engaged and I wouldn't want to ruin that for her. It would destroy her, and I never want to hurt her. She really does love her boyfriend. I just don't think that they're right for each other. "Good show Abigail," I say as I touch her lightly on her shoulder.

"You too," she replies. "Hey, what was with that guy? I overheard the drama going on." She sounded concerned about it.

"Just another asshole treating me like I'm his own personal whore. Damn it, I'm not a whore, I'm a dancer!"

"Yeah, I must say he did seem a little creepy," Abigail says with concern in her voice still. She's has such a caring personality, I have no idea why she even bothers being my friend. I'm sure she has the same daddy and abandonment issues that all people in this industry possess but she never lets it get to her. She really is the exception to the rule, the golden example of stripping through college. Whatever it is she sees in me, I'm probably better off not knowing.

"So are you on lap dance patrol or was that your last dance of the night?" I ask while I take off my undergarments.

"Jasmine called in so I'm covering half of her shift tonight. We should be getting off at around the same time," Abby said.

"Well at least you got a decent shift. Last time I covered for Jasmine, I got stuck with a Tuesday afternoon," I say and roll my eyes.

"Let me take a guess, James showed up, didn't he?" She asks.

"Don't be such a bitch, Abby. You know very well that James shows up every Tuesday afternoon wearing the same blue sweat pants and shirt after he gets off from work."

"I know. He usually asks for me by name. He doesn't even get that we all know he's jerking off while dancing for him...so disgusting!" She smiles. I know deep down she likes the attention.

"Well I should be off at eleven. Do you want to grab something to eat after we're done tonight?" I ask.

"Sure, as long as I get to pick the place this time," Abigail replies.

"Back to The Den, eh? You and your greasy spoon diners. I don't understand the appeal in them," I laugh. She is always satisfied with the simpler pleasures in life. Two more squirts of cherry body spray and I'm ready to work.

11 P.M.

"I can't believe that guy offered you two hundred dollars just to let him blow his load on your feet! Men are nasty!" Abigail says. She takes her panties off in the drab dressing room

"I can't believe I let him!" I reply. I realize that this is what my life has come to. Hoping she had forgotten or changed her mind about The Den, I ask her, "So where do you want to go to eat? I'm not sure what places will let me in dressed in my jammies."

"If you don't mind me asking, what's the deal with that?" Abigail asks. "Did you get out of bed late?"

"Yeah, something like that. Hey, let me coke up really quick and we can get out of here."

"Okay, fine, whatever. Just meet me at my car," Abby says. I know it bothers her a lot but it's not like I'm doing heroin or anything like serious. I snort the last bit of my stash and head out.

I open the back door of the Pink Triangle. The metal bar across the exit door is cold, matching the weather as I step outside. I see only four cars in the parking lot, and one of them is mine. There's a white car with a busted headlight. I guess Abby didn't realize it was out. I walk over to her car across the parking lot and get a bad feeling. I step to the passenger door and open it. I sit down into her car and close the door. I hear the click of the doors locking.

"How dare you embarrass me like that!" a man's voice yells. Oh shit! I reach around to turn the dome light on and notice his silhouette illuminated by the moonlight. I see his lips, his mustache, the center of which is white, the rest brown. I notice his pants are pulled up above his gut with his shirt tucked in just like the man who... Oh shit!

"Look, I'm really sorry! I didn't mean to hurt your feelings. I was just having a really..." He cuts me off.

"So you didn't mean to spit on my money and throw it back at me? Huh? Did you? You owe me, bitch!" he says.

"Oh, I don't owe you shit!"

"I think you do, and I think you agree," The man says, revealing the pistol in his hand. He lifts himself up off the seat and pulls his pants down, exposing his small ~~and wrinkled~~ wrinkly penis.

"Suck it," he says, loosely aiming the gun at me.

"Fuck you, asshole! I'm not a whore and I'm not a slut either."

"Would you rather be a dead saint, or my whore for a little bit? I swear to God, if you make me lose this hard on, you'll be eating ~~three~~ bullets before I can get it back up." I sit in complete shock for a moment. The despair in my eyes gave him my answer. "That's a good girl," he says while patting me on the head like a dog. I begin to cry. Pull yourself together, I think to myself. You know if he sees you crying, he's going to lose his hard on. I lean over his lap, and a couple of tears that I couldn't manage to hold back fall from my face and into his pubic hair.

His erection is staring at me, inches away from my lips. It makes me want to vomit. I take a deep breath. This is the bravest I've ever had to be. I place my hand at the base of his pubic bone, brushing away his brittle hairs. I put his cock in my mouth and close my eyes as tight as I can.

He thrusts his hips upward, trying to force me to go down farther on him. I oblige him. The back of my tongue touches the tip and I can taste his semen. He's either about to finish, or he jerked off earlier to make sure this took a while. It tastes absolutely horrible, like rotted milk in a dead refrigerator. He starts moaning but all I hear is the phlegm caught in his throat as he tries to clear it.

He places one hand on the back of my head, putting pressure on it. He forces my head to slide all the way down his cock. It hits the back of my throat, making me gag.

"Mmm, yeah baby, choke on it. Choke on that huge cock," he says, obviously satisfied with what he's making me do to him. I can't do this anymore. I just want to die. This has to end. I try to pull my head back to stop myself from gagging. He doesn't let go of my head. The pressure he places on my head feels like a coconut in a vice.

I can't do this any longer. He may still kill me even when

he finishes. He knows I can identify him. If he was going to kill me, I'll give him a reason to remember killing me. I chomp my front teeth hard into his penis. My incisors shred his delicate skin as I bite harder, making sure to grind it between my jaw. I can taste his blood as it fills my mouth. I clench and jerk my head away as hard as I can. I can feel the skin stretching and tearing before it comes off in my mouth.

He raises his gun to my face and with his finger wrapped around the trigger. I look up at the glare on his eyes. They are filled with of pure contempt that is rarely seen outside of movies. I spit the loose skin into his shabby face. His eyes widen in horror. As it bounces off his left cheek, I reach for the gun in his hand. I grab the barrel double fisted and raise it upwards. He punches me in the jaw. Does he think I've never been hit before? His grip loosens from the pistol. I pull it back against the passenger window just out of his grasp. I twist my body around, and slam my back hard against the passenger door to make space between us. I guess my time spent pole dancing wasn't a waste after all. I place my heel into his throat. He gasps for air. I think I hit his Adam's apple but it's difficult to tell under his mounds of neck fat. I straighten my leg out, snapping my knee into place like cheap furniture. The impact smashes his head against the driver window.

I straighten my arm and squint as I take aim at the fat fuck. "I'm not your whore, asshole!" I pull the trigger. The bullet pierces his skull as if it had been a cudgel. Blood splatters over the entirety of the interior. Fragments of skin, brain, and skull decorate the inside of the car.

His body convulses. I had heard this happens. The body continues to function after the person has died. I can relate too well. It's just different seeing it in front of you instead of feeling it inside. Each limb starts jerking erratically, as if he hadn't died but his life spread into his limbs.

"Stop it!" I pull the trigger again. This time it goes through his neck, hitting his jugular. Blood sprays into my face and mouth. The flailing continues. I snap my finger around the trigger once more. The shot hits him in the heart. I squeeze it again and again, until his body becomes still.

I wipe the gore from my face, not recognizing what chunk of his body it was. I unlock the door and get out, soaked in the fluids of a rapist. I stumble slowly towards my car across the abandoned parking lot.

When I reach my car, I hear a muffled cry. I look over my hood and see her through the window covering her mouth. She's is hysterical. Fuck Abby, why did you have to be here? I tap on the window. She doesn't bother to look at me. She's still sobbing into her hands with her head resting on her furry pink steering wheel cover. I reach for the door, and startle her. "Please don't. Please don't kill me, okay? Please don't," Abby pleads with me.

"What? Why would I kill you? It's okay, hun. Shhh, it's okay," I say, trying my best to comfort her but it's only making matters worse.

"You...you...killed someone in that car, didn't you?" She looks at me, scared. The last thing I ever want her to be is afraid of me.

"Yes, but it's not what you think, Abby. The fucker raped me at gun point! Wouldn't you do the same thing?"

"I don't know. I don't know if I can believe you, but that doesn't matter. You're going to kill me if you want to. I always liked you, you always treated me nice. Most people make fun of me behind my back for being so nice, but you never did Candy, you never did."

"I know. I've always really admired that about you, Abigail. You always had to do whatever you could to make things right."

"You're right, I have to do what's right," she said as she picks up her phone and presses three numbers. "I have a murder to report. It happened behind the Pink Triangle. I saw my friend kill someone in a car. I heard the gunshots and she stepped out of the car."

"What the fuck are you doing?" I frantically grab the phone from her ear and throw it across the parking lot. The battery dislodges from the device as it skids across the pavement.

"I'm sorry Candy but I have to do what's right. I thought you were going to kill me!" Abigail's eyes start to well up again.

"What the fuck did you just do to me, Abby? Why the fuck did you just do that to me? I didn't do anything wrong, Abby! He fucking raped me!"

"Then the courts will sort it out, Candy. If you didn't do anything wrong, then nothing will happen to you." How could she do this to me? I guess I never meant as much to her as she did me. Tears fall from my eyes, mixing in with the blood, creating in a cocktail of pain and violence.

"Abigail, I loved you. You've always been there for me. We never tell the people we care about how much we actually care. I loved you more than just as a friend. You were my motivating force for trying to straighten up my life, Abby, but it doesn't matter now."

"Why not? Why doesn't it matter now?" She looks up at me, her hands still on the steering wheel.

"You were the only person in my life that never did me wrong," I say.

Bang.

Bang.

Click.

Click.

Click.

Click.

Click.

Click.

I throw the pistol in the air, hoping it hits God. I sit on the hood of the car and wait for my destiny. There's no use in running. No one is going to take me in and hide me. I just killed the only person that would have taken me in. I don't want to be on the run for the rest of my life. That's not the life I want to live. This life isn't the life I want. I wanted her life. The life I just took.

When I was a little girl, I had the same dream every Saturday night. I had committed some horrific act by accident and I was on the run. All I could remember when I woke up was the feeling of being helpless and utter disparity of the dream. I had the feeling that the world was searching for me, and even though it wasn't my fault, they still wanted me dead. Dread is the only way to describe it, I guess. I never realized that the ordinary world is what I should have feared, not this.

I can see the blue lights reflecting off of the stones from the building next to me. No sirens echo. I suppose they wanted to creep in and catch me but I'm still here. I look over my shoulder at Abigail's lifeless body. She was so young. I know I should feel worse for taking her life. Her jaw had slacken, tears from when she was alive streaked to her dead face. They drip down into the car seat like melting icicles after the first day the sun breaks.

I place my bloody hand on the windshield. I love you Abigail. I regret a lot in my life, but I would have regretted nothing more if I had not told you that I loved you. The officer grabs my hand from the windshield. The perfect imprint of my bloody hand stains the window. He wrenches my arm behind my back, the other soon follows.

The Body of Sandra "Candy" Collins

The bullet hit Sandra in her right temple. She had been afraid of The Innocent in her last moments, alive, her face reflected that. She braced for the shot when the bullet hit her. Her head slumped forward and her arms went limp. Her eyes were tightly shut, as if they were glued together. Her tears mixed with the blood from the wound in her head making a mixture you could only expect from a cheap horror film. Blood dropped from her temple, staining her tank top.

The guards entered the room, with only the sound of their boots slapping against the concrete floor. The Innocent, visibly shook, continuing to hold the gun with a two handed death grip. The Short Guard tried to grab the gun.

"Hey, let go of the goddamn gun before we blow your fucking head clear off your shoulders! Got it, sissy-ass bitch?"

"Y-yeah, I got it, I mean, sorry sir." The Innocent trembled as he let go of the gun, giving it to the guard. The Short Guard emptied the bullets from the chamber, dropping them onto the floor. He handed the gun to The Pacifist. The Tall Guard grabbed Sandra's lifeless body beneath her arms and wrapped his hands over her breasts, squeezing them.

"Hey, I told you her tits were real. I fucking knew they were."

"Fuck off, and let's get her the hell out of here. Maybe Steve will want to fuck her before we throw her on The Pile,"

223

The Short Guard laughed as he lifted Sandra's feet from the floor. The thought of The Pile made The Innocent's stomach turn. He felt even sicker to his stomach at the thought that he just sent one of his fellow inmates to The Pile. As the guards carried her out, Sandra's bloody hand smacked across the only door that led out of the execution room, leaving a nearly perfect imprint of her palm on the glass.

The Pacifist

The Innocent pounded his fist against the table, vibrating it so violently that it shook the security camera that peered down at the inmates from the corner of the room. He clenched his eyes together, much like Sandra had done moments ago and hammered his fists against the table again. He opened his eyes, not only to realize that his hand was bruised from hitting the table, but also that he was shaking uncontrollably. "I didn't mean to kill her. I didn't want to! You motherfuckers made me do it! You made me do this! It's not my fault, it's yours!" Spit flew aimlessly from his mouth as The Innocent yelled at the guards from behind the wall. Snot poured from of his nose as he thrashed against the table once more. "What the fuck did you make me do? Why did you make me do this? Why don't you just fucking kill us already? Why do you want to put us through this motherfucking shit? Why don't you just come here and kill us like fucking grown-ass men? You don't have the fucking balls to do it, do you? I bet you fuckers don't even have the balls to step from behind that glass and shoot any one of us square in the motherfucking skull," The Innocent screamed as the door clicked. The Short Guard steps into the room, the door slamming shut behind him. Seconds later a sound of a click was heard as The Tall Guard locked them back in the room.

The Short Guard grabbed The Pacifist with one hand

on the shoulder and the other around his neck and threw him out of the chair, his face sliding across the floor. The Short Guard sat down in the newly vacant chair and removed his riot mask and threw it in the corner, nearly hitting The Pacifist.

The Innocent recognized him immediately from the scar on his left cheek. He was the guard who escorted him from the courtroom to his cell. "You're not talking so tough now are ya, you fucking punk-ass bitch?" The Short Guard said lighting up a cigarette. "You want to give me the chance to take one of you guys out personally, it'll be my pleasure. It's been so hard letting killers kill killers, just sitting here watching. It's my job! I should be the one taking you assholes out. But let me tell you motherfuckers something, I'm walking out of this room. You may get the chance to ice me, but I promise you, you're not gonna succeed."

The Innocent's tears quickly turned to anger. "Is that what you fuckers think about back there? Just waiting for your chance to pick us off one by one, and how great it would be to take us out? How are you any better than us? How are you any different than us? This isn't your life, this is your job. It doesn't give you the right to play fucking God. If you don't like this shit, then quit. You guys are just sick, power hungry perverts who get off on thinking about killing people. Fuck you!" The Innocent said. He threw his head back and spit on The Short Guard. The Short Guard didn't even flinch as the spit hit his shoulder.

"Well, seeing as it was ~~badtie's~~ baldy's turn with the gun, and I'm taking his place, ~~I guess it's~~ that would make it my turn now, ~~isn't it?~~" The Short Guard said with a smug smile across his face. "You've made my choice a little easy too, haven't you? It made me so happy ~~dragging~~ to drag your ass ~~to~~ into a cell, you prick. It'll be even better dragging your body out of this room." The Short Guard took the gun from the table and put a bullet into the chamber. "I don't get any enjoyment out of this, but can you even comprehend what our job is like? We get paid a shitty wage to babysit fucking derelicts that should be killed the minute they are found guilty. Do you understand how frustrating it is being around people who don't think twice about taking the lives of others but don't want ~~yours~~ their own to be taken?"

The Pacifist was sitting in lotus position in the same place he had been thrown by The Short Guard. The Pacifist spoke up. "Some of us know what we did was wrong, and are just seeking redemption. Everyone has done actions they are not proud of. We just need time to understand what it was that we did was wrong," ~~he said.~~

"Don't even for a second act like stealing a piece of gum from the gas station when your ten is the same as murdering your family," The Short Guard replied.

"In a way they are. They are all acts that we know to be wrong but we commit them anyway because of the reward.

Obviously, murder is a bit harsher than stealing candy, but the premise remains the same."

"You know what, justify all the fucked up shit you people have done any way you want, it doesn't make you anything more than a bunch of shit stains in the underpants of the world."

"So...why are we doing this?" The Terrorist asked.

"What the fuck are you talking about? You're doing this because you want out of ⟨?⟩

"That's not what I meant. Why was this decision made? We've seen the news, of the thirty four states that still have the death penalty, twenty nine sentenced them to life, three states did mass executions, and one did medical experiments. Why are we the one state chosen for this sick game?"

"Ratings. Why the fuck else do you think?"

"What?" The Innocent asked surprised, his jaw agape.

"What the fuck do you think we have the camera in the corner of the room for? So we can see you? That's what the one way mirror is for, fucking retards. The camera is for our lovely viewers at home. Really, you all didn't figure that out yet? Think of all the lives you ten miserable fucks have ruined, about the families you've ruined. They deserve to grieve. This is the world getting to see your asses get murked, and you deserve it. All of the terrible shit you admitted here, the world now knows," The Short Guard said.

"Please just fucking stop! I didn't even kill my family. All of my friends and family are going to watch me be murdered for something I didn't even fucking do! How is that fair? How is that justice?" The Innocent slammed his fist down against the table again.

"You didn't have much problem killing that whore, did you? Your family isn't even alive to see it. You killed them. You seemed pretty natural with that gun to me. You're a motherfucking murderer, just deal with it. You're also more than likely going to die in this room where everyone can watch," The Short Guard said as the buzzer went off. "The good news is Steven, is that you're helping me out by playing this game." The Short Guard lifted the gun at The Hitman and gave him a nod. He braced the gun with his second hand to ensure he had an accurate shot.

-Click-

The Hitman

The Short Guard stood up and walked over to The Hitman. He whispered something in his ear as he set the pistol in front of him. He then walked back to his seat.

"What the fuck was that about?" The Innocent asked.

"None of your fucking business," The Short Guard shot back at him.

"Oh, so you can tell him whatever the fuck you want. You don't have to obey the rules we have to follow, huh? You can just waltz down to his end of the table without anyone blowing your head off, right?"

"Yeah, that's right," The Short Guard replied.

"And why the hell is that? Are you too afraid to play the game for real? Don't think you can handle it without needing an advantage?"

"Nope, just need to make sure the game is being played fair."

"Well then, what the fuck did you say to that freak?" The Innocent asked.

"He told me if I shoot him, I won't walk out of here alive," The Hitman said grinning. "The problem with that, Johnny Law, is that I don't expect to be getting out of here alive. I've never had the chance to kill a cop, and now is going to be my only chance." The Hitman picked up a bullet from the table and put it next to his ear. "It's a helluva thing, piggy. That bullet just told me that he really wanted to kill a cop too," The Hitman snapped the chamber shut.

"You motherfucker, you know you won't do it. You even so much as raise that barrel at me, and I'll blow that mohawk off your skull," The Short Guard said grasping his standard issue pistol at his side. "I don't mind playing fair, but I'm not letting a punk like you take me out."

"Well you don't have to worry about that. I'm not the revenge type. There isn't any satisfaction from killing a cop. In the rights of fairness I think you should answer some of the questions we had to answer."

"Like what?"

"If you were on death row, what would be your last meal?" The Hitman asked.

"I wouldn't be on death row with you cocksuckers," The Short Guard replied.

"That's not the question. What would you have if you were on death row?" The Hitman reiterated.

"Your head on a fucking platter. Next," The Short Guard said.

"C'mon, play along. What's it gonna hurt? You wanted to be one of us bad enough that you sat down in one of our chairs."

"Alright. I'd probably say chicken parmesan over penne pasta and garlic bread. It really doesn't get much better than that, boys."

"What's the worst thing you've ever done?" The Innocent asked.

"Fuck you."

"We all said it. What's the worst thing you've ever done and never got caught for? It's not like anyone is going to arrest you for anything you say. Even if they did, they can't give you the death penalty for it."

"My brother. He, um, killed himself when we were in school. I was a senior, he was a sophomore. He was turned down by some chick he had a boner for so he killed himself over it. I wish I could have told him not to worry about it, that it's not the end of the world. I wish I could have told him that he'll move on, that it's not worth fucking dying over. I never had the chance to do that. I miss the little fucker and I never really showed it. That's the worst thing I've ever done. It's part of the reason I'm here. Any other stupid questions you want to ask?" The Short Guard almost began tearing up before he realized he couldn't do that in front of them.

"Wow, I'm sorry. That must be really terrible, to lose your little brother, especially at that age," The Innocent said.

"Yeah, no shit," The Short guard shot back.

"What made you want to be a prison guard?"

"I was a good kid growing up. After what happened with Matthew, my life went a little crazy. I knew something drastic was going to have to happen in my life. It was either going to be law enforcement or I was going to end up a criminal. Luckily, I picked the right one. It could have gone either way. Maybe in another life I could be in your shoes right now"

"What are you going to do after this is over?" The Innocent questioned The Short Guard.

"Who knows? I'm sure the media will want interviews."

"So you're just a fame whore?" The Hitman said with a smirk.

"I don't want the fame. I don't want the notoriety. It's about a promise that I made to him, I don't expect you to understand it, but this was supposed to happen. I want people to know the truth. Who the fuck knows, maybe I'll write a book about it."

"So it's not about the fame, but about the money?" The Hitman fired back.

"It's about letting other people know about a unique experience. What's so wrong with that? Y'all are a bunch of cocksuckers. The Prairie Dog Killer wrote two fucking books after he was convicted. No one asked the family of the victims to write a book, just the asshole that sliced their throats and inked them," The Short Guard explained.

"How many serial killers can you name? Now how many victims of serial killers can you name? Isn't it fucked up that we can't remember hardly any of them, but we glorify the sick fucks that did it?" The Short Guard was interrupted by the buzzer. The Hitman took the gun in his hand, deciding what he was going to do. The more seconds that passed, the more nervous The Short Guard became. He didn't want to die in this room of convicted murderers. The Hitman raised the gun towards The Terrorist and once again gave him a nod of respect as he pulled the trigger.

R.L. Murphy

-Click-

The Terrorist

The Hitman gave The Terrorist another nod of respect and slid the gun towards him. Without saying a word, The Terrorist placed another bullet in the gun and set it on the table in front of him.

"Don't think we haven't realized your strategy. You're just being the silent guy to try to squeeze on through to the end," The Short Guard said.

"That freak has used every turn of his to try to take me out. That's not exactly flying under the radar. How many times have you had a gun pointed at you today?"

"None as of yet, but I also didn't kill any American soldiers now, did I?"

"Fuck you."

"Fuck me? No fuck you! I'll take your Allah lovin' ass out so quick the seventy two virgins won't even be expectin' you ya," The Short Guard said.

"I hope you die," The Terrorist replied.

"We all die, asshole. Some of us just deserve it more than others."

"Like your brother? Did he deserve it?"

"Don't you even start motherfucker!"

"I'm glad he's dead. The little pussy deserved it. Killing himself over a girl, he must have had a small dick."

"Shut the fuck up about Matthew before I end this

game for you right now!" The Short Guard shouted.

"Killing me won't change the fact that it's your fault that he's dead."

"I'm warning you for the last time, asshole." The Short Guard unclasped the button on his holster and placed his hand over the grip of his pistol.

"We both have a gun, pig. Mine may only have three bullets, but how many times do I need to squeeze it before your head comes flying off?"

"You do that and you'll never get out of here alive. I'll make sure you get ripped in half before I throw you in The Pile."

"The Prairie Dog Killer was right...we're all dead. None of us are getting out of here alive. There is no game, is there? This is just some fucking circle jerk going on with the CO's giving us a bit of hope before we're taken out, isn't that right?"

"Trust me, if we wanted you dead, we wouldn't have waited. In fact, it makes us sick just knowing that one of you fuckers will be alive and free after what you've done. You deserve to be tortured and killed, but instead you get a chance to go fucking free," The Short Guard replied. "We had to pull major strings to get this together. This whole thing is important to me, important to Matthew."

"You also convict innocent people. Do you ever think about all the innocent people you've put to death?"

"It's a damn shame but I didn't convict them. I'm not a

judge, and I'm not on a fucking jury. I'm just a guy trying to make things right, that's it. I'm happy they got rid of the death penalty, last thing I want is more innocent people to die. This is just a job, I'm just trying to support my family."

"You couldn't keep your brother alive. How do you expect to support your family?" The Terrorist mocked.

"Do you think you can just get away with saying that shit?"

"No, I know I'm going to die so I might as well tell you that your brother deserved to die because he had such a shitty brother," The Terrorist said.

"I'm giving you one last chance to back the fuck off."

"So you're telling me I get to call your brother a miserable faggot who's rotting in hell forever because of you one last time? How very generous of you," The Terrorist laughed.

"You motherfucker!" The Short Guard drew his gun from its holster. The Terrorist had already taken aim at his head.

"If you raise that gun one goddamn inch, I'll blow your face clean off. Put your gun back in its holster. At most it will take me four squeezes of this trigger to send you to see your brother. You of all people should know I won't hesitate to kill a man in uniform." The Short Guard begrudgingly brought down his pistol, placing it back in its holster, keeping his eyes on The Terrorist. "You need to know, I don't want to kill you, because you don't deserve to die like this. You're not one of us. You're not good enough to be one of us. You deserve to be eaten by that cannibal rotting on 'The Pile', as you so pleasantly put it." The buzzer sounded, breaking up the glare between The Terrorist and The Short Guard.

The Terrorist lowered his aim of the gun at The Pacifist who was still sitting in lotus position in the corner of the room. He looked to be meditating. "Hey, I'm going to shoot you. Are you going to, you know, stop doing that?"

"I see no reason why I should," The Pacifist said.

"I suppose, that's your choice," The Terrorist said. He pulled the trigger of the half loaded gun.

Russian Poker

-Click-

The Innocent

The Innocent had a bullet ready in his hand even before The Terrorist handed him the gun. The room hadn't been this quiet since The Short Guard first sat down with the inmates. His presence had initially started a lot of commotion but now that he had finally settled in, The Short Guard felt like one of them.

"There's a real good chance this thing is going to go off in the next few minutes. I don't really care who I take out. What will you offer me for your chance that it won't to be you?" The Innocent asked. He didn't look at anyone in particular but merely glanced at everyone seated around the table.

"I won't shoot you next round," The Hitman offered.

"You aren't going to shoot me next round anyway. You've had a hard-on for The Terrorist since minute fucking one. Try again," The Innocent said. He wasn't convinced by The Hitman's offer.

"If you kill The Terrorist right now, I'll need to move onto someone else. Shoot him and you're safe the next round regardless of if it goes off or not."

"I won't shoot you in the next two rounds," The Terrorist offered.

"I don't trust you."

"But you trust that freak?"

"With my life? Fuck no! To keep his word? Yes. He's a son of a bitch but he's a son of a bitch with honor," The

Innocent said, giving The Hitman a nod.

"Three rounds, three rounds I won't shoot you," The Terrorist said grabbing his hair in frustration.

"The higher your number goes, the less likely I am to believe you're going to keep your promise. Let's say I take you both up on your offer, would you both keep your promise?" The Innocent asked.

"Yes."

"Yes."

"Well that certainly limits my options now, doesn't it? What are you willing to do for me, piggy?"

"I don't got to do shit for you. If you kill me, Seth is going to be in here to blow your fucking brains out, simple as that. If you want to live, you need to kill one of these two fucks or the fuck in the corner trying to hide," The Short Guard said. Without opening his eyes or breaking his concentration from his meditation, The Pacifist spoke.

"I'm not hiding from anything. If you wish to shoot me, then shoot me," he said.

"We all know there's no reason to kill you. You're not going to kill any of us. No one wants you dead and you know it."

"Maybe no one wants me dead because I'm the only one that realized we're already dead," The Pacifist replied.

"No, it's just that it lowers the chance of us being

murdered the longer you stick around," The Hitman said.

"So, there are no other offers on the table?" The Innocent asked.

"What else do we have to offer? We have no other bargaining chip. We don't have any material possessions in here," The Hitman said.

"What about our possessions outside of here? This is on television, right? So that would make it legal if we say we want all of our stuff to go to someone," The Terrorist said. "So how about this: If you don't shoot me this round, I won't shoot you the next round and you'll get all of my possessions."

"Great, so I'll get some AK-47's and a pile of turbans," The Innocent remarked.

"I bought a Ford F-150 two months before I was deployed, and my apartment is full of electronics."

"What if I don't live? Then what happens?" The Innocent asked.

"If we're both dead then it won't matter. Otherwise it'll just go to whoever it would normally go to."

"Seems reasonable," The Innocent said, thinking the offer over.

"I'll do the same. I promise not to shoot you next round. I don't keep many possessions besides my house and car, but I have a gun collection you could easily sell for half a million," The Hitman said.

"Deal, but just know I am going to sell them," The Innocent said.

"Just know, if you go back on your deal, we're going to kill you," The Terrorist said. The Innocent remained silent. For the next couple minutes everyone sat silently. The buzzer went off.

"Well, I guess this is where your game ends," The Innocent said staring The Short Guard in his eyes. He picked up the gun and aimed it at him. He watched as the look in The Short Guard's face changed from smug to defeated.

"Hold up just a second. I'll give you what you want. I'll give you what you really want," The Short Guard said, his face now grinning.

"Enlighten me," The Innocent said with the gun steadily pointed at The Short Guard.

"I'll find who murdered your family," The Short Guard offered. The Innocent swung his arm around, aiming at The Terrorist. He stared into the eyes of The Short Guard.

"Deal," The Innocent said with a grin.

Russian Poker

-Bang-

The Story of Khad Al-Ali

"Why must I choose to kill to survive?"

I wake up blindfolded and tied to a chair. This wasn't quite the trip to Iraq I was expecting. I didn't realize I was naked until a small draft of cold air hits my body. The smell of the room is putrid. If I'm going to be killed in here, I don't want to see it before it happens. Judging from the smell of this place, I wouldn't be the first.

I sense someone walk up behind me. I hear someone unsheathing a sword. My suspicions are confirmed when I hear him chuckle while he cuts the rope away from the chair I am in. I stand up, take the blindfold off, and face his direction.

The person who cut me loose is covered from head to toe in black garb. I'm breathing heavy. He can tell that I'm about to do something drastic. He lifts up his hand with his palm facing me, gesturing for me to calm down. In his other hand, he unveils a gun that he has concealed inside his garment. He extends the barrel of the gun towards me, enticing me to take it. I oblige.

"Calm down, sir. There's no need to be scared, you're in no danger," the man says.

I point the gun at him, aiming between his eyes. "What's going on, what is this?" "It's time you make a choice. Where does your loyalty stand? Turn around," the man in the black garb commanded. As I look to the other side of the room, I see two people naked, tied to their chairs in the exact manner I was mere seconds ago.

I don't recognize the captives tied to their chairs. I can see them breathing, but otherwise they aren't moving. The man in the black garb puts his arm around my shoulder and whispers in my ear. He whispers that he wants me to choose. He wants me to decide which of the two captives to kill. He tightens his grip around me, getting close enough so I can feel the warmth of his breath caress my ear. The man in the black garb says that I have the opportunity to ask the captives three questions each. Afterwards, I must make my decision. He says that if I choose to kill myself, then both captives will be set free. The man in the black garb steps out the room, leaving me to decide the fate of the two captives

I take the blindfolds off both captives, but decide to leave them tied to their chairs just in case. In case of what, I don't exactly know. The captives look at me with the same wide eye glare I showed moments ago. I tell them to calm down, and reassure them that I'm not going to hurt them. After saying it, I realize that I am lying to one of them. They are both men. They are both tan but I can't tell their ethnicity. One of the men has dirty blonde hair, so I assume that he's American.

I tell the captives I have a few questions to ask them. The blonde guy has a worried look on his face. I assure him that this is not an interrogation and don't even think of it that way.

"Tell me about yourselves," I ask. The blonde one speaks up first.

"My name is Josh Scout. I drive a supply truck between army bases. I'm not even enlisted. I'm just a contracted worker from Oregon. I have a wife and two boys back home. Tyler just turned four last week, and James is six. I play guitar, and love old samurai movies," Josh says. For a few moments, there is a long standing silence. The other bound man speaks up.

"I guess it's my turn now?" he says. "I mean, I don't know what to say really. My name is Bobby Hampton. I was born and raised in Louisville, Kentucky, but my family is from Iraq. I came back to visit my grandparents who stayed behind here. I don't know exactly what happened but apparently a car bomb went off outside their house and insurgents stormed the neighborhood for prisoners. Next thing I know, I'm tied to a chair with a hood over my head. I got divorced two years ago. She couldn't have kids, but she made sure to take everything I had during the split. She took my house, my car, my savings account, and most of my retirement money."

"What did you get?" I asked.

"The only thing I got that mattered to me...Tyson, my dog. He got me through everything. He was a gift from my ex-wife when we got married. I told her I would get married but I wanted a dog. He was there with me when I was unemployed.

He was there when I was addicted to prescription drugs, and he was there with me through my divorce. This has been the hardest time of my life because Tyson isn't here with me. I don't have any children but Tyson I love like he was my own child," He said.

I don't know if that helped me make my decision or not. It's not going to be an easy decision no matter who I choose. Hell, is there even a right decision? I guess it doesn't matter who it is...except to them, it does. Neither of them wants to die. They both have something to live for. There has to be some way out of this.

I ask my next question, "What's your biggest regret?"

"That I never opened the restaurant I always wanted to open," Josh Scout confesses. "It was going to be like one of those hibachi places. You know, where they cook in front of you, but with barbecue instead of rice and shit."

"What about you, Bobby?" I asked.

"My biggest regret? My biggest regret is that I never married the woman that I truly loved. When I was twenty four, I couldn't work up the nerve to ask her out. She was a coworker, and I never thought she'd ever want anything to do with me. Little did I know, she liked me too, but it was too late. She thought I wasn't interested in her so she moved onto someone else. I wonder how my life would have turned out if I just had the balls to ask her out. I probably wouldn't be here, would I?" Bobby said.

I don't know if this is helping or not. Questioning them is not making my decision easier, but I know the only way I'm going to justify this is if I find a fault in one of them.

"What's the worst thing you've ever done?" I ask. "And don't bullshit and say you've never done anything wrong. This is your chance to get anything off your chest. Josh, what's the worst thing you've ever done?"

"I cheated on my wife. I don't mean that there was some sort of one night stand. I mean that my wife, Tabitha, was the other woman and she didn't even know it. Once Tabitha became my main woman, I picked up at least one, and sometimes up to three other women. The kicker to the whole thing is that I never felt bad for it until one of them found out. I only cared then because I really didn't want any of them getting hurt. I just wanted to have a little fun," Josh said.

"So you're just finding girls to hook up with?" I ask.

"Fuck no, it's a whole relationship. They all thought we were exclusive, and none of them knew about each other except for an occasional mix-up. I bought two girls engagement rings one Valentine's Day. I knew I wasn't going to marry either one of them but you know...it's what I had to do to keep them going," Josh said.

"Would you do it again?" I asked.

"I mean, I don't feel bad about it so I guess I would do it

again. I probably would be more honest with the other girls. Most of them wouldn't have minded, but I knew it meant a lot to them to think they were the only ones."

"Bob, what about you?" I asked.

"Worst thing I've ever done? God, I don't know, man. I haven't done anything that terrible, I guess. I guess the worst thing I've ever done was when I was going through my divorce. I logged into her e-mail before she even thought about changing her password and saved all of her personal information. That's how I found out about the other men she was talking to," Bobby says.

This definitely isn't making it any easier. Bobby doesn't seem like a bad guy. He's just a guy who loves his job and scared out of his fucking mind. Josh has done some awful things but he has a family. I don't think I can kill Josh. I don't want to take a father away from his children. I have to kill Bobby...unless I kill myself. Then they are both free.

The door creaks and the man with the black garb steps back into the room. "Have you made your decision?" he asks.

"Yes," I say, gripping the gun as tightly as I possibly can. I step in between the two men. Bobby starts to cry. I raise the gun to his head and press the barrel against his temple. Bobby pleads to me between bouts of crying for me not to kill him. He really hasn't done anything to deserve this. I remove the gun from Bobby's head and jam it into Josh's. I pull the trigger.

The sound of the gunshot echoes louder than the actual shot itself. Brain and skull fragments mix around in a pool of Josh's blood gathering beside him. I drop the gun and begin to untie Bobby. "Don't worry about untying him, I'll get it," the man in the black garb says as he walks towards me. He picks up the gun I dropped on the floor and offers the gun back to me. "You might need this," he says. As I reach out for the gun, the man in the black garb turns around and places the gun to Bobby's temple. Bobby's eyes widen in fear.

The man in the black garb pulls the trigger. Bobby's body slumps over. I stand up and lunge at him. I use what little wrestling experience I remember from high school and pull his legs from underneath him. I pin down his hand that is holding the gun and use my other hand to rip the gun from his grip. The gun slides across the room, stopping when it hits Josh's foot. The man in the black garb slams his forehead into my nose. I feel it crack and blood from my nose drips onto his garb. I raise my arm above my head, ready to drop an elbow in his face. He reaches inside his garb, pulling out a knife as I come down on him with my elbow.

He jabs the knife into my shoulder and rolls out from underneath me. I pull the knife out and feel every inch of the steel exiting my body. I charge at him, clenching the blade as hard as I can. The next thing I know I'm on the ground. I don't feel like I fell but I felt my ankle pop. I can already feel it swelling.

"You're not getting up," the man in the black garb says. "The knife was poisoned." As if he knew when the poison would take effect, I start feeling myself become drowsy. My limbs are getting heavier. I close my eyes, feeling my consciousness slipping away from me.

When I wake up, my whole body hurts. Blood has dried, causing my shirt to stick to my skin. When I try to move my arm to separate the two, I notice I'm tied to the chair again. No, not tied, just placed in the chair. Why would they go to that trouble?

I hear voices whispering in the distance. I hear the familiar sound of several boots shuffling across concrete. The boots are getting closer. I hear the clink of a soda can as it bounces off the floor. The room immediately fills with smoke. I'm lifted from the chair and slammed face first onto the cement ground. I feel my nose breaking again with another crunch, and another onslaught of blood.

"Boy, why the fuck did you do it?" the man behind me says. "Colonel, we got'em! The target is subdued."

"What are you talking about? Did you get him? Did you find him?" I ask.

"We should have known not to let some rag head over here like this," said one of the other men.

"You're going to go to prison for a long time. If they

don't execute your ass, that is," another man chimes in.

"Hell, he's lucky we don't take him out right here after all the fucking trouble he's caused," a woman's voice says.

"What did I do?" I ask.

"Don't play dumb, cocksucker. We found the gun right next to you. You really can't expect us to believe you didn't kill them, can you?" the woman says.

"I...I killed one of them. I killed the man named Josh, but the man in the black garb killed Bobby," I say.

"The same type of bullet was used on both of our guys. They came out of the same gun, and no one else is here," one of the men says.

"Our guys? They weren't military, I swear!"

"God, you really don't know what you've done, have you? The two you called Bobby and Josh were spies. You successfully killed two undercover agents collecting intelligence from terrorist units," the man explains.

One week later

No one believed my story, no matter how many times I tried to get them to understand. They gave me the same response over and over again. They wanted me to admit that I was a spy for the terrorist unit, and that I found out that Josh and Bobby were American spies, tortured them, and then killed them. They never gave me any information on Josh or Bobby, but I wonder if anything they told me was true. I assume it was all a lie until I think back about how serious Bobby seemed about his dog. There was something about Bobby's voice when he talked about his dog that I knew there must be some truth to it.

A man in an army uniform tells me to come out of my cell. Great, another fun day of interrogation. I walk down the same corridors I've been lead through for the past six days now. The ceilings are low with barely any lighting, and the smell of mold permeates the hallways. They take me into a new room today. I've never been in this door, the third door on the right, but it's what I feared most...the water-boarding room.

The man in the army uniform instructs me to sit down. I sit in the only empty seat around the lone table in the middle of the room. There are two new men already sitting at the table. Just like everyday for the past six, I don't recognize the new set of interrogators. They already had confession papers on the table for me to sign. They go through the same lines of questioning as previous days. They ask me what I was doing in Iraq, who I was working for, and why I won't just admit I was a spy. I tell them I refuse to admit it because I'm not a spy.

I ask them questions about Bobby and Josh, but they refuse to answer anything about them. I ask about procedures about becoming a spy for the United States. I ask them if the background check goes as deep as knowing if they own pets. One of them says nothing, while the other tells me that it's scary how much information is tracked on you without you even being aware.

They ask me what it's going to take for me to sign the confession papers. I think about it. I really think about it. They're either going to keep me here and torture me until I sign them, or I'm going to admit to something I am not and didn't do. I might as well get the answer to the one thing I'll never know unless I ask.

"I want to know about Bobby, or at least the guy who told me he was Bobby," I say.

"You know we can't tell you anything about our agents, alive or dead," one of the interrogators replies.

"Look, Bobby said something to me that seemed plausible. I believed in his story, and the reason I didn't shoot at him was because of that story. I'll sign the paperwork if I can ask you three questions, but you have to answer truthfully. Deal?" I ask, trying to negotiate with them. The two men interrogating me are stunned by my response. I guess most people in this situation just ask for money, or maybe a possible way out. I just wanted the truth.

"What kind of questions?" they ask in unison.

"I just want to know about them, about Josh and Bobby. I want to know about the real people, and not the people they told me about," I said.

"Fine. There are a few things we can't divulge. We

won't tell you the names of their wives, children, addresses, or anything you could use to track down their families," the interrogator to the left says. I nod in agreement. "So you have three questions, then you sign your confession. What's your first question?"

"Did Josh really cheat on his wife?" I ask.

"Wouldn't you? He had the coolest job in the world. All agents have the ability to charm anyone into anything. It's nearly impossible to not abuse that power. To answer your question more directly...Josh wasn't married. Josh never cared for people much. He kept to himself mostly. The only social reaction we ever saw him have was when we found out about his YouTube channel about fishing," the interrogator on the right answered. "What's your next question?"

"Did either of them ever kill anyone? I don't need specifics of who or what or why, but just if they've murdered before," I ask.

"If you think it's any easier to cope with the fact that you've killed an assassin, it isn't. A human life is a human life, and you took two of them. Josh never killed anyone, it really wasn't his thing. He was really good at getting information out of people. He didn't need to resort to lethal action. Bobby, on the other hand, we've had some problems with. Don't get me wrong, he always got the job done...always, but he liked to use any force needed to get out of a bad situation. So yes, Bobby was a trained killer," the man on the left answers. "What's your last question?"

"Is Tyson real?" I ask. "Bobby talked about his dog being the only thing he cared about. I need to know if that's true."

"He never could keep his mouth shut about that dog. Yes, Tyson is his dog. He's had the damn thing for about the last seven years," the man on the left says. "Since we've answered your questions, that means it's signing time." The man on the right hands me a pen. It's heavier than I expected. The ink flows so smoothly from it, I start to think it must hold some sort of magic. I guess if you're going to sign away your freedom, you might as well do it with a nice pen.

"I need to make a request. Any money that I have in my possession, I want to go towards taking care of Tyson. We all may be guilty, but that dog isn't. That dog is the only true innocent here," I say.

"We can arrange that. There will be additional paperwork to deal with that aspect of it, but I don't see any problem with it," the man on the right says. "Anything else you'd like to add?"

"I didn't want to kill him but I don't regret my decision. I did what I had to do," I say as I stand up and wait for whatever I'm about to face.

The Body of Khad Al-Ali

Even though The Innocent didn't bother looking while he took aim at The Terrorist, he managed to hit his target perfectly. The Short Guard was relieved the second the bullet came out of the gun. Khad, however, was not so enthralled. The bullet struck him in his throat. Blood gushed from the wound as he fell out of his chair and onto the concrete floor. Khad's blood covered the floor, pooling beside where his body laid. The sound of gargling as Khad tried to utter his last words was the only thing heard within the room. The remaining four people waited for Khad to die, trying their best to ignore the sound of his death.

As the noise came to an end, The Innocent looked over at The Short Guard and said, "That could have been you on the floor. You better keep your promise. You better not sleep until you find the fucker who did this to my family. And if I make it out of here, I'll be doing the same."

"When I had you in handcuffs and was carrying you off to your cell, I knew it didn't feel right. I knew deep down I was throwing an innocent man into a cage. You have my word that I'll do the right thing," The Short Guard said. The Tall Guard stepped into the room.

"Okay, you've had your fun. Back to work. I need help moving this camel fucker to The Pile," The Tall Guard said. The Short Guard nodded to The Tall Guard and picked up his riot mask that was still lying at the feet of The Pacifist. The Short Guard tapped The Pacifist with his foot while he put on the mask. The Pacifist stood up and took his seat. The guards picked up Khad's body and carried him out of the room.

The Pacifist

The Innocent handed the gun to The Pacifist. He was smiling for the first time since the night his family was murdered. The Pacifist emptied out the three remaining bullets from the chamber of the gun and placed them on the table in front of them. He picked up a bullet from the table and placed it into the gun. "Why are you so happy?" The Pacifist asked.

"I don't care whether I live or die, I just want the rightful person to be in prison for killing my family. They need to experience the pain that they've put me through," The Innocent explained.

"If you do make it out of here and find the killer, will you kill him?" The Pacifist asked.

"Yes," The Innocent replied.

"Would you kill his family?"

"No, the family didn't do anything. Mine didn't either, but I'm not the monster that he is."

"But you'd still take their father away from their family?"

"He doesn't deserve to live."

"Who does? Who has led a life so pure that they deserve the life that has been given to them? Life is the most astonishing gift to ever have been given. None of us deserve it, but we're still given it."

"He especially doesn't deserve it."

"What if it's not a man? What if it's a woman? Would you kill a woman?"

"If that woman killed my family, yes."

"And if it was a child? Would you kill a child?"

"No."

"And why not?"

"Are you seriously asking me why I wouldn't kill a child? They're innocent, they're pure, and they don't understand the consequences of what they do."

"Some adults don't either. Does it make it right to kill them? Would you kill a mentally challenged adult?"

"No for the same reason."

"So there are no pure adults? Gandhi wasn't pure? Mother Teresa? Jesus?"

"I'm sure Gandhi and Mother Teresa did things that they weren't proud of. And Jesus, who knows? That was a long time ago, you know?"

"Interesting. Why do you hate adults so much?"

"It's not hate, we're all just selfish assholes. We don't truly care about anyone else."

"I see. And that makes it okay to hate your fellow man?"

"I never used the word 'hate'. I've lost faith in humanity. Man killed my family, man destroyed my life, man sentenced me to death, man put me in this room, man tried to kill me."

"I can see your point, I suppose. Just keep in mind the only difference between children and men is time," The Pacifist said. The buzzer goes off as if The Pacifist had planned for it as he finished his sentence. The Pacifist raised the gun, closed his eyes, and pulled the trigger.

-Click-

The Hitman

The Hitman caught the gun as The Pacifist slid it down the table to him. He loaded the second bullet into the chamber nonchalantly. "So how do you guys see this playing out?" The Hitman asked. "This is how I see it going down. I'm not likely to kill anyone this round. If I do, it has to be you, Mr. Peace, since I promised I wouldn't shoot you this round." The Hitman pointed at The Innocent. "If I do that, I'm not sure I would kill you. You deserve to get out of here more than I do. I would let you kill me and you'd be free to find the killer of your family."

The Pacifist interjected. "I don't believe you're going to keep your promise. I think the next time you're holding the gun, you're going to shoot and kill an innocent man. Then you're going to kill me, unless I kill you first."

"What the fuck are you talking about?" The Innocent piped in.

"I'm a pacifist, I don't believe it's right to kill a man, however a man who breaks his word is no longer a man," The Pacifist said.

"Well then, don't worry about it. I'm a man of honor, my word is my bond. If I kill someone this round, it will be you," said The Hitman.

"A man of your word? You're a freak, yes. A vagabond, definitely. But a man of your word, no," The Pacifist said.

"I've never killed someone who didn't deserve it. Killers, thieves, mobsters, those are the people I've taken out. I kill as a precise art, not out of rage or other emotions. I would never dream of killing my family, I love my family." Tears began to swell around The Hitman's eyes. For the first time since entering the room, he was beginning to show some emotion. "Family is all that you have in life."

"It's nice to say that but we will see if you keep your end of the bargain. Even if you don't, you still have a fifty-fifty shot at getting out of here."

"No I won't. If I break my word, I deserve to die and I expect one of you to do it."

"I hope that's true."

"Yeah, so do I," The Innocent said. "It's my ass you guys are talking about killing."

"I suppose you do have a small stake in your demise in this instance," said The Pacifist.

"How do you see this lethal game of chess playing out?"

"Well, I hope to get the gun next round, I kill you" The Innocent said and pointed to The Hitman. "Then it's a coin toss whether I kill you or not, baldy."

"A coin toss is not needed," The Pacifist stated. "I won't kill you. You deserve this more than anyone else around this table. As I've said before, I've already come to peace with my own death. If it comes down to me and you, you've already won. Just promise me, either of you will make it painless for me. I don't want to be suffering with a hole in my neck."

"Precision isn't a problem for me," The Hitman said.

"I'm a foot away from ya, I think I can handle that much," The Innocent agreed.

"Good."

"Can I ask you something?" The Hitman said looking at The Innocent. "So, I mean, you have no idea who killed your family? Usually these sorts of deals are a domestic thing, or at least a close friend or something."

"No idea. The only thing I'm remotely sure about is her family has thought about killing me just because of how I treated her, but they wouldn't kill her. Not only that but who could kill their own granddaughter? They loved Sarah as much as we did. I mean, who would want to kill a fucking child?"

"There's a bunch of sick fucks out there," The Hitman replied.

"So if someone paid you to kill a woman or child, would you?" asked The Pacifist.

"A woman? Sure. If women want equal rights, I'll be sure to give it to them. A child? That's completely out of the question. Unless the kid is pointing a gun at me, then it's a matter of survival."

"H-have you ever killed a child?" The Innocent asked.

"Part of my job is never talking about specific jobs."

"Even if this is your last chance to clear your conscience?" The Pacifist asked.

"What makes you think I have one? You don't need one of those as long as you live by your own code of morals."

"And you think you do?" asked The Pacifist.

"Of course. I wouldn't do anything against my morals. I don't let my emotions get the better of me."

"Yeah, you're also a fucking kid. Wait until you have a wife, then talk to me," The Innocent said.

"First off, I'm twenty four and not a kid. I don't really need any females in my life. Complicates too many aspects of life," The Hitman replied.

"I didn't realize you were a fag," The Innocent laughed.

"Neither of you have any room to talk. You beat your wife, and you killed yours. Sharing your life with a woman hardly ever turns out good. I'm not gay, but I'm sure you can imagine the kind of girls that I attract," The Hitman said.

"I'm sure they're a bunch of freaks in the sack, am I right? Real dick wizards, I bet," The Innocent said raising his eyebrows.

"The crazy ones always are, and those girls are certainly that," The Hitman continued. "You can't trust girls who have a chemical imbalance, and in my line of work, trust is everything. I couldn't keep my line of work from someone I am with. That would be against my morals, so instead, I just choose to be by myself," The Hitman said. The three remaining men sat in silence until the buzzer sounded.

The Hitman picked the gun up from the table. "I think you're smarter than anyone gives you credit for," he said as he aimed the gun towards The Pacifist. "Good-bye."

-Click-

The Innocent

The Hitman slid the pistol towards The Innocent. He caught it easily. The Innocent eagerly placed another bullet in the gun and set it on the table in front of him. "So, how did you get into your profession?" The Innocent asked The Hitman.

"You should know by now, I'm not going to tell you how I got in," The Hitman stated.

"But if someone wanted to get into that profession, how would they do it?"

"There's really only two ways. The first is to join the military. Try to be either a sharpshooter or a navy SEAL. After you get out, they always come lookin' for guys like that."

"What's the second way?"

"The way I did it."

"How's that?"

"You think I'm going to tell you just because you asked again? Why all the questions? Thinking about a new profession?"

"Not really, but I always wondered how people get jobs like that, you know? You can't really just apply for them. Is there any sort of interview process?" The Innocent asked.

"Yeah, it's called 'kill someone for free and give us the murder weapon so we have something over your head in case you get any crazy ideas.' Once you're in, you're in. How the hell do you become a hotel manager?"

"By going to community college and partying your way to a business degree."

"That sounds better than having a premeditated murder lingering over your head."

"Yeah it does, but doesn't get you nearly as much pussy as killing people for a living," The Innocent remarked.

"The only ladies in my life are my guns," The Hitman said.

"So do you do the thing where you wait on a rooftop for hours with a sniper rifle waiting for a congressman to step out of a limo?"

"I'm not getting into specifics, but I practice for any situation that I may find myself in. So use your imagination," The Hitman said. "I will say this, I've been in situations not too far off from mob movies. Hollywood isn't too far off."

"No shit?"

"Not a drop of shit."

"So what was your weapon of choice?"

"You mean what is my weapon of choice? There isn't one. The biggest mistake you can make is being reliant on the same weapon. Never leave a calling card. I'm not a serial killer, I'm a professional. It's simply about using the most precise tool you have available so you can get the job done as discreetly as possible."

"Sounds like being a prostitute."

"I'm okay with being called the prostitute of death. I've heard worse titles in my life."

"Like politician or lawyer?" The Pacifist interjected.

"Yeah, something like that," The Hitman said. "What about you? You said you were some sort of architect, right? What the fuck is that like?"

"Pretty boring, actually. I made the blueprints for things that will probably never be built. I designed bridges for cities that can't afford to build the structures, but wanted the plan ready in case they ever do. The exciting part is actually constructing a bridge, not designing it," The Pacifist said. He felt as if he had given the same speech thousands of times.

"Kind of ironic, isn't it? You constructed things, brought things to life, and I destroyed them," The Hitman said.

"Yeah, I guess it is, but I think our motives are very different."

"I don't kill because I enjoy killing. I kill because the money is good and I'm good at it. I don't think it's any different than you wanting to be an architect."

"I suppose that's fairly accurate. I just picked a major in college that paid well," The Pacifist replied.

"See? So what do you think will happen as soon as one of us gets out of here? Do you think there will be news crews, or a press event, or something?" The Innocent asked.

"Assuming they just don't throw us all in The Pile, I'm thinking they just let one of us out. I'm sure there will be some media attention, like when any murderer gets off the hook initially. People will be outraged and will want to know how we feel about it, and if we're lucky, eventually no one will remember our name until we're a question on Jeopardy or something," The Hitman said.

"That wasn't exactly how I intended to leave my mark on life, but it's better than nothing, right?" The Innocent said. "A lot of people get in this world and don't do shit. No one remembers them."

"Yeah because that's how you want to be remembered? The guy who murdered and got away with it? It's really easy to be remembered notoriously. However, it's much harder to be recognized by doing something great," The Pacifist said as the buzzer rang.

"Well, I'm sorry. I don't want to do this, but I think it's the right move for me. I hope you understand," The Innocent said to The Hitman. He nodded his head as The Innocent picked up the gun and aimed it at The Hitman. He pulled back the trigger with more confidence than ever before.

Russian Poker

-Click-

The Pacifist

The room was silent as The Innocent handed the gun to The Pacifist. The Pacifist put the fourth bullet into the gun and set it down on the table. The Innocent finally broke the silence and spoke up. "How does it feel knowing that the gun is probably going to go off and it's just delaying us?"

"Every time I pull the trigger, I assume it's going to go off. If you don't aim at anyone, you're not going to kill anyone. Wasting your time is better than me trying to kill you, is it not?"

"I suppose it's a good alternative," The Innocent said.

"Then you should be happy that I'm doing what I'm doing."

"Until you decide to shoot one of us instead. Then we won't be so grateful," The Hitman replied.

"How many times do I have to prove you wrong before you believe me?" The Pacifist asked.

"Until you prove me right, which means I won't know because I'll be dead. The only other way I'll believe you is when you're dead."

"Well I expect an apology when I'm dead."

"Unfortunately I don't think I'm going to get the chance."

"Hey man, seriously, I've never seen someone doubt another person so much in my entire life. He's a pacifist, not OJ fucking Simpson," The Innocent remarked.

"I know people. I know how to read people. I'm not wrong. The sooner you realize it, the longer you'll live. I may be an asshole, but I'm a asshole with honor," The Hitman said.

"Don't judge people by their words, judge them by their actions," said The Pacifist. "I'm the only one in this room who hasn't killed someone else, and yet I'm the one you judge."

"You're the only one that hasn't killed anyone in this room yet."

"And I never will."

"Do you promise? Would you shake on it? Would you put your honor on the line?"

"I'd put my life on the line."

"Well that's good to know because it is," The Hitman replied.

"I'm not going to live because that would mean I would have to kill one or both of you. Seeing as how I have no intention of killing anyone, I have no life. How many times do I need to tell you that I'm already dead before you believe me? Do you keep on forgetting? I know you're not dumb, you pride yourself on your intelligence. However, you put too much stake into your intuition and not enough on logic."

"Will you two really just stop it? He's either going to kill one of us, or one of us is going to kill him. Does it really fucking matter at this point? Does honor really mean shit in this room? If your head gets blown off, no one is going to talk about your fucking honor. They're going to talk about some asshole freak that got his head blown off on live television," The Innocent said. "I mean, seriously, we're sentenced to death, and now we don't expect to die? Are you that fucking stupid that you don't see that? Are you really trusting them to do what they say they're going to do? They have a pile of people who were sitting right next to us just moments ago. You really think they care about us? You really think that they give a shit at all?"

"It's not about accepting our fate, it's about being positive. Giving out positive energy returns it to you. I know that more than likely I'm going to die, but I have hope I'll make it out of here. The world has a way of returning the favor," The Pacifist said.

"Get the fuck out of here with that Anthony Robbins bullshit. There's no karma, there's no divine retribution, shit just happens. Simple as that. If this world is anything but chaos, explain to me babies dying, starvation, or people murdering their families," The Hitman said looking at The Pacifist.

"That's not me any longer," The Pacifist replied.

"But it was you. You are still that same person, and that's why I think you're going to try to blow my brains out when that buzzer goes off."

"I am physically in the same body but my spirit is new."

"Keep talking that bullshit. It's the same brain and the

same body. You're a murderer and you'll always be a murderer."

"Nothing you say is going to make me shoot anyone. I'm stronger than that, and it's not because I don't want to break my word. I don't want to break my morals. You can't break that, the guards can't break it, no one can," The Pacifist said as the buzzer went off.

"You're wrong. You've already broken yourself," The Hitman said.

"I'm not wrong. All I can do to prove you wrong is die, right? Is that what it's going to take? Then so be it." The Pacifist picked up the gun from the table and placed it to his temple. "This is what it's going to take, is it? I'm going to have to die to prove that I'm right?"

"I'd certainly have no choice but to believe you," The Hitman replied.

"I'd rather go by my own hands than give you the satisfaction of killing me," The Pacifist said as he closed his eyes. He pulled on the trigger slowly. He hesitated. The Pacifist said, "I hate that it was you who saw right through me." The Pacifist extended his arm, putting the gun up to the temple of The Innocent.

"Wait, what?" The Innocent said. The Pacifist pulled the trigger.

-Bang-

The Story of Steven Jones

"What do I have to do to prove my innocence?"

My fist lands squarely upside her jaw. I knew in that very instant my marriage was over. I couldn't apologize for hitting her again this time. You can't keep apologizing again and again. She admitted that she has been fucking around on me. I can't blame her. I knew she would, I just never thought she would do it like this. Sure, I've probably spent too much time with Steve down at the bar, but I'm still a good father. How dare she say otherwise?

Yes, I freaked out when Sarah was born. Especially with the complications Sarah had. Girls are prepped their whole lives to become mothers. I had never been through this before. I didn't know how to react or think. I needed time to myself so I could sort out how I felt.

When you see your child for the first time, it's supposed to be perfect. How was I supposed to react when I saw that she was missing fingers? The doctors told me it was a birth defect from the sleeping pill my wife was taking. It hadn't been tested quite as well as they thought previously. Thank you FDA for fucking up my child's life. Before she was born everyone told me as long as she has ten fingers and ten toes that nothing else mattered. Fuck you! They don't understand what it's like bringing a child into the world with half her hand missing.

I could tell that all of our friends and relatives that came to visit us while we were at the hospital just stared at Sarah's hand. They never mentioned her beautiful red hair, or her crystal blue eyes. They would say how adorable she was, and end up walking away. All they could see was her deformed hand.

She's packing up now to leave me while I stand frozen in the place where I hit her. I tell her to not bother, and that I'll leave. I call Joe, but he doesn't answer. I go to the bar where I know I'll find him. There are only a handful of people there when I arrive and I know them all. By the time I sit at my regular spot at the bar, the bartender has poured my shot of scotch for me already. He can tell it has been one of those nights. "How's it going tonight, Joe?" I ask. Joe shrugs.

"Another rough night?" Joe asks while placing the bottle of scotch back behind the counter.

"Yeah, you can say that, another rough night. She finally left me, Joe. Can I get another scotch?"

"Yeah, no problem, but take it easy tonight, okay? You don't need to overdo it. No worries, right?"

"Yeah Joe, no worries," I repeat. It's never easy to tell what the truth is when your only friend is also your bartender. Will our friendship dry up when my money does? He doesn't give a shit about me. Why would he? I'm just the guy who gives him money to listen to my problems.

I need a place to stay but I can't just ask him. I look up at Joe, trying my best to look distraught.

"You don't need to say anything James. You can stay at my place tonight, but just for tonight. My wife will light my balls on fire if I let you stay longer."

"Thanks Joe, you're the best."

I guess I better go upstairs above the bar to his place. I leave a twenty on the bar and Joe hesitantly gives me the key for upstairs. Not that I blame him. The stairs creak a lot while I tiptoe my way to Joe's apartment. The only other time he allowed me to stay at his place was the night I met her. I thought this was a once in a lifetime shot, and I needed to take advantage of it. That night I never thought in a million years I'd end up hitting the women in the blue dress with the red hair that I obsessed over. I guess Hitler never grew up thinking he would murder seven million people either.

The place hasn't changed much since the last time I was here, and that was five years ago. Why didn't she leave a long time ago if she was so unhappy? Did she stay just to wait until I fucked up somehow? Does she want to make sure she gets custody without much of a fight from my lawyer? Bitch! I'm not even sad about her leaving. I'm just frustrated that the family I pictured in my head isn't the same as I see with my eyes. Why couldn't we just make it work? We both wanted it to work, right? Why is this so hard?

7 A.M.

What time is it? I must have fallen asleep while rambling to myself. Ugh, the clock says seven. God, I hope Joe doesn't have his clock set right. I better get dressed. I walk into the kitchen and check the fridge. I need to see if Joe has anything to get the nasty aftertaste of scotch off my breath. No dice. Just lemon juice. Well, I guess, bottoms up. No matter how many times I do this, I never get used to it.

Joe is still sleeping. I don't want to cause an argument between him and his old lady so I better go. I fold the blanket neatly and leave it on the couch with the last twenty I have in my wallet on top of it. I try to open the door as quietly as possible but it still squeaks.

I never get used to seeing the bar closed from the inside. It's like one of those places that seems sterile without the people who gather there. It's like a kindergarten classroom during winter break, all signs of life on the walls but none between them. I leave through the emergency exit on the other side of the bar. Stepping outside, the air is cold. I walk around the building and open my car door. I always leave it unlocked. It hasn't been broken into yet.

I have no idea if my wife will even let me in our house. I at least need to pack my car with my shit, that is if she hasn't burnt them or decided to spread my shit across the yard like confetti on New Year's. She may have already went to her mother's house like she did the last time she left me. I see that her car is in the driveway. No matter, her mother may have picked her up. I know that she doesn't like to drive when she is upset.

As I walk up the porch steps, I grab my keys from my pocket and unlock the front door. At least she hasn't changed the locks yet. I creep through my cookie cutter suburban home as if I am an intruder. "I'm home," I say sing songish as if I were a dad from a sitcom in the 50's. No one answers. I didn't expect her to rush for me and embrace me, but a response from her would have been nice. I turn on the light and see the shadow of her head on the floor in the kitchen. She must have drank too much and passed out. I can't say that I blame her for that. I better check to make sure she's not choking on her own vomit. We lost Hendrix that way, we don't need to lose her that way too.

Stepping closer to her, my heart begins to race. Her body lies still on the lemon colored linoleum of the kitchen floor. I grab her shoulder and turn gently turn her over. I...I...I...NO! She...killed herself. She told me that she would do it if I ever left her. Every moment we've shared together is gone. Every moment we were going to have together now gone. The vacation we talked about taking to Europe...gone. I didn't know I was this bad to you, Sweetheart. I love you with everything I fucking am! How am I such an asshole that I made her do this? What did I do? I'm sorry Baby, I didn't mean this. I didn't mean to hurt you like this. It was an accident. I promise I never meant to hurt you. I just wish I could apologize to you and make everything right again. I wish I lived my entire life differently. I wish this could have been different. I would have never touched you or alcohol if I knew this would happen.

Wait, I don't see a gun in her hand. There's no gun anywhere! Oh my God...I count her wounds. She was shot six times. One in her eye, one in her forehead, and four in her chest. Oh no...Sarah! I run upstairs to her room. Her door is still closed. I close my eyes, grab the doorknob, and slowly turn it. The door opens. I shut my eyes as I step into her room. Tears blinding me, I open my eyes. Without looking any closer, I knew what had happened. Motherfucker! Why? Why is this happening to me? I gotta call the police. I need to catch this fucker.

I call 9-1-1. It rings, but no one answers. I try again, and again, and again. On my tenth try, someone finally answers. I don't get five seconds into the conversation before the phone cuts off. I look down at my cell phone. The battery is dead. I can't stand to be in this room or this house right now. I need to leave.

I drive to the police station, running every red light and blowing through every stop sign along my path, hoping someone will just run into me so I can be put out of my misery. I can't live without my daughter and now she's gone. I'll never see her graduate. I'll never walk her down the aisle. I'll never hear her tell me she loves me again. She's gone.

I make it to the police station in record time. I leave the keys in the ignition as I rush for the entrance. I approach the receptionist and frantically tell her what happened. She instructs me to slow down like I'm some sort of crazy person. Why isn't she listening to me? Why doesn't she care that my daughter is dead? An officer finally greets me and I tell him what I found when I got home. He asks me to give him my statement and I obey. He writes it all down, and tells me he will check into the matter. He leaves me in the meeting room where I gave him my statement. Two hours later, they place me under arrest.

One year later

They told me later that day that they found the gun used to shoot my wife and my daughter in my daughter's bedroom. Nothing was stolen from the house. The neighbors heard us arguing the night they were murdered, and Joe refused to testify that I stayed the entire night at his place. Joe didn't believe I didn't do it. He thought I went back home in the middle of the night and did the deed. Everyone turned on me. My family, my co-workers, my friends...all of them. Everyone that would have supported me in the courtroom I was being convicted for killing. As the judge gave his verdict, he told I was

awkward

an abomination. He said I not only robbed my family of their lives, but also my daughter of her innocence. We're both innocent, Sarah. We're both still innocent.

As I'm being taken back by the bailiff after sentencing, I hear my wife's family screaming at me, murderer, killer, monster. I stay remain silent and keep my head down. I can't let them see me cry. They'll think I was guilty, Sarah. I can't let them see me cry.

Sarah, I promise I'll find him. I'll hunt down the person who did this to you and your mother. I may be in prison, but I'll find him, and I promise I'll make him pay for stealing your red hair, your blue eyes, and your beautiful hand...away from this world and away from me.

The Body of Steven Jones

The Pacifist smiled as the body of ~~James~~ *Steven* Jones slumped over the table. The Hitman was angry, but he was more disappointed by The Pacifist's decision. He ~~was~~ *had been* hoping ~~to be~~ *he was* wrong about him. The Hitman was merely baiting him, believing The Pacifist would succeed in staying true to his word. Maybe this had been his plan the entire game? Or maybe it had been a split second decision on his part? Regardless of The Pacifist's intentions, the outcome was still the same.

Neither man said anything as the guards stepped into the room to dispose of ~~James'~~ *Steven's* body. The Short Guard bent down, grabbing the body up from under ~~his~~ *Steven's* arms and dragged him out of the room while The Tall Guard stood over the remaining two inmates and watched. The Short Guard had taken ~~James~~ *Steven* Jones from the courtroom to his cell, then from his cell to the execution room, and now from the execution chamber to The Pile. ~~The cycle was complete.~~

The Hitman

The Pacifist smiled as he emptied the bullets out of the gun. He passed it across the table to The Hitman. "I hope you're happy with yourself," The Hitman remarked.

"You should be thanking me. He would have killed you. Instead, I killed him for you."

"And you expect me to believe you're going to go back to pacifism after this? I'm not that fucking stupid."

"No, of course not," The Pacifist remarked. "I will do what I need to do in order to survive. When it comes down to it, man will always do what is needed for survival. I am a pacifist, yes, but pacifism is about opposition to war, not to violence. The murdering of my family was what led me to pacifism, but what I did just now wasn't an act against it."

"There is no way I'll let you out of here alive. It won't end like that. You don't deserve to live after what you just did," The Hitman said.

"Who does? You? The reason we are here is because we deserve to die. The only guy who may not have deserved it was the man I just shot. And who even knows if he was truly innocent. My intuition was telling me that he was guilty of the crimes he was convicted of."

"Fuck you and your intuition. I'm here to win this game just as much as anyone else that is or was here, but I guarantee you, I'm not letting you leave here alive," The Hitman said.

"That may not be your decision to make."

"I'll make sure that it is."

"What are you going to do, shoot me? Are you going to keep pulling the trigger until you kill me? Just so you can be killed by the guards?"

"If that's what it takes. I'm not afraid to die either."

"Christ, you should be. You're only twenty-six years old."

"I'm twenty-four. Age doesn't mean anything when your job is to take someone out. All that matters is how well you do your job. You're not going to resist pulling the trigger on me now because of my age, are you?"

"Of course not," The Pacifist replied.

"Then we have to do what we have to do. Do you even feel bad for what you did?" The Hitman asked.

"I never feel good about murder, no. I'm not one of those disturbed individuals who gets their rocks off by taking someone else's life."

"But do you feel bad?"

Yes, I do."

"But you don't regret doing it, do you?"

"No."

"He was fucking innocent," The Hitman said slamming his fist onto the table.

"He killed someone, he's not innocent. Maybe he was innocent when he first entered this room, but he wasn't when I shot him," The Pacifist replied.

"Is that how you justify it?"

"I don't need to justify what I did. Would have you preferred I shot you?"

"No, I wish you would have stayed true to your word and shot the ceiling instead."

"I think those days are over for me."

"I hope all of your days are over."

"Well it's a fifty-fifty shot. Flip a coin and let's see who goes free."

"I wouldn't be opposed to it instead of wasting all this time," The Hitman said staring into the eyes of The Pacifist as if he were piercing his soul with his eyes.

"I still expect to die, that didn't change."

"I'll make sure that happens."

"I don't doubt that for a second."

"Good. I will enjoy killing you."

The buzzer sounded. The Hitman raised and aimed the gun instantaneously. Without hesitation, The Hitman pulled the trigger.

-Click-

The Pacifist

The Hitman slid the gun to The Pacifist without breaking eye contact. "I can't wait to see you bleed," The Hitman said.

"There's no strategy involved now. This is all about luck. There's no reason to try to intimidate me," The Pacifist replied.

"I'm going to enjoy watching the guards pull your lifeless body into The Pile."

"What are you going on about? Why are you now starting to hate me?" The Pacifist remarked as The Hitman's breathing became heavier. He kept his eyes locked onto The Pacifist's.

"Now it's personal."

"How could it be personal? What have I done to you?"

"You don't deserve to know."

"You're the one being aggressive towards me. I'm the person who does actually deserve to know why."

"The only thing you deserve now is death," The Hitman replied.

"We all deserve death. That's the point of us being here, remember?" The Pacifist said.

"I can't let you out of here alive, and you won't."

"What are you talking about?"

"That's the interesting thing about being a contracted killer, you know how to spot other people in your field in public. I've hired a friend of mine on the outside to kill the person who walks out of here if that person isn't me. The kill won't be immediate, that would be stupid. You'll live your life day by day not knowing when the bullet is coming, and when it does, you'll know it."

"You're just trying to scare me, and it's not working. Scare tactics might work on someone with weak will, but that is not me. I welcome death, I'm not afraid of it. So should you."

"I welcome nothing but life. Nobody is certain what happens when you die. All that we know is that life is worth living, and that everyone is afraid of death. Even the most devout Christian fears death. That's proof enough for me that we should be enjoying every second of life with what we actually want to be doing," The Hitman said.

"You're a miserable fool. Why do you refuse to seek harmony within yourself at the expense of a good time?" The Pacifist asked.

"You're a man who sits and ponders, and thinks that's what life is. I'd rather be better than you than to think I'm better than you. What have you done with your life? I've accomplished more than you could dream of and I'm half your age. I've been around the world, I've seen Easter Island, and I've stood in The Coliseum. I've stood at the top of Machu Picchu. What have you done? You read books, you think about things no one can prove, and you killed your family. That's all your life is and ever will be. How can you possibly say you have led a fulfilling life?"

"You're a pretentious fucking punk with tattoos on your face. Who are you to tell me what I've done with my life? It's my life, I can do whatever I want with it."

"Of course you can, but just because you did what you wanted doesn't mean you didn't waste it. What did you want to do that you never did do?" The Hitman asked.

"I never went to Hawaii. I always wanted to go but I never did," The Pacifist replied looking a bit downtrodden. "What about you? What do you regret? What did you want out of life that you haven't gotten?"

"The only thing I ever wanted out of life you took away from me," The Hitman snarled at The Pacifist. He peered up at The Hitman puzzled.

"I really don't know what you're talking about. What could I have possibly taken away from you?"

"Danielle."

"What? How did you know her? How did you know my wife?"

"I knew her because I loved her," The Hitman said grinding his gums together.

"There's no fucking way... You got to be bluffing."

"When I found out you killed her, I purposefully allowed myself to get caught. Do you actually think I'd be stupid enough to get caught because I wasn't careful? I wanted to get caught! I wanted to get close enough to kill you. I wanted to kill you in prison. I couldn't let anyone else do it. I never got the chance. That was my mistake. I'm going to rectify it here, for Danielle's sake," The Hitman said.

"You son of a bitch!" The Pacifist said. As if on cue the buzzer went off. The Pacifist didn't hesitate. "You are the one who ruined my life! You're the reason why I'm in here, you fucking freak." Tears cascaded down his eyes as his arms trembled while he aimed the gun at The Hitman. The Pacifist pulled the trigger.

-Bang-

The Hitman

The Pacifist grinned as the blast from the gun echoed off the concrete walls. He never noticed how loud the blast was until it was he who was pulling the trigger. He saw The Hitman fall forward onto the table. A pool of blood oozed from the right of his head. The Pacifist didn't see the hole from the wound, just the blood as it gathered. The guards didn't enter the room.

"They must be taking their time," The Pacifist thought to himself. Then he noticed it, he saw that he was still breathing. All he needed to do was just wait until The Hitman bled out. It would only take a few minutes. The Hitman sat up, holding his right hand over his left shoulder. "Give me the fucking gun. It's my turn."

Shocked, The Pacifist reluctantly passed the pistol across the table to The Hitman. He thinks that if he bleeds out before the buzzer goes off he's not in any danger. He couldn't tell how serious the wound was but if it's a shoulder wound, it probably was not life threatening. The Hitman caught the gun with his left hand. He opened the chamber, unloaded the bullet that was still in it, and placed a new bullet in the gun with his left hand. He did it with such ease that The Pacifist didn't doubt he had been trained for this.

"This is your fault. This whole thing is your entire fault," The Pacifist said. "You're the reason I'm here, you're the reason

I killed my family, you're the reason I had to endure all of this bullshit. Why did you do it? Why did you have to see her? Out of all the people you could have fucked, why did it have to be my wife? Why did you have to take her away from me?" The Pacifist continued talking as if there were no one in the room.

"I didn't choose her. I loved her," The Hitman said, blood soaking through his shirt and dripping down his fingers.

"Fuck you. How can you say you loved a married woman? What did I ever do to you? Was I so fucking terrible that you had to decimate my life?"

"It's really none of your business," The Hitman remarked.

"Bullshit! It's all my business! You're talking about my life. You're talking about my family. You're talking about everything I had. And you dare to tell me it's none of my business? You little shit! I'm going to rip your head straight off your body."

"It'll be hard to rip my head off when you're dead."

"Why? Why would you do this to me?" The Pacifist asked.

"Why did you do it to me? You knew there was someone else out there who cared about her, but you didn't care, did you? You were never home. You weren't a husband to her. You weren't even a father to your own fucking kid. I was more of a father to her than you ever were."

"How dare you fucking tell me what kind of husband and father I was!"

"I'd say strangling your wife makes you a pretty goddamn shitty husband. You don't even deny you were a bad father. You're such a piece of shit. I don't care what kind of enlightenment you hide behind, you've always been a piece of shit. Nothing has changed."

"You've never been a father. You don't know what it's like. I'm not trying to say I was the best father ever, but I was a father and I loved her," The Pacifist said.

"Killing her sure is a funny way of showing it," The Hitman remarked.

"I didn't have a choice."

"When the option is killing your own fucking child, you always have a choice."

"I wouldn't have been in that position if you didn't fuck my wife!"

"It's funny how people don't take responsibility for their own actions."

"I feel the same way," The Pacifist said. The two stare at each other in silence. The Pacifist was hoping The Hitman would just keel over dead from his wound in his shoulder while The Hitman hoped The Pacifist realized how he had wronged him. The buzzer rang. The Hitman raised the pistol. He could feel the bullet in the chamber as he pulled back the hammer.

"Any last words?"

"Whether you kill me or not, you've ruined my life," The Pacifist replied.

Russian Poker

-Click-

The Pacifist

The Hitman passed the gun to The Pacifist, surprised that his intuition was wrong. He knew the bullet was in the chamber, but it wasn't. The Pacifist placed another bullet into the chamber and snapped it shut.

"I didn't ruin your life, you ruined it yourself," The Hitman said. "You were the one that fucked up your own life. You weren't there for her. All a woman really wants is someone to pay attention to her. If you weren't going to do it, someone else was willing. Just because that someone was me, doesn't mean it was my fault."

"If that's true, why didn't you kill me first? Why did you kill The Gangster and then go after The Terrorist?" The Pacifist questioned him.

"They were the real threats, you weren't. I knew I'd get my shot at you if I could take out the real competition. It may be a game of luck, but that doesn't mean there's no strategy. I mean your strategy worked pretty damn well, didn't it? Appear harmless then at the last minute, kill someone unexpectedly. You can't tell me you're not here because of it," The Hitman said.

"It wasn't a strategy. I wasn't going to kill anyone, and it wasn't an act. I didn't feel the need to kill until that very moment. It was almost like I was fighting with myself," remarked The Pacifist.

"Killing is part of human instinct. It's who we are. It's who we've always been. Humans are destroyers of life. No one had to teach us how to kill, it's always been within us. We condemn those who kill, yet we all feel that need. There's no man who hasn't thought about killing someone, but they don't. They let made up societal laws get in the way of it, but it's part of who we are. Now we are locked away in cages like zoo exhibits for just being a human being as if we're too dangerous to be contained."

"Then why are you mad about me killing my wife? That's the problem with kids, you never think about how things actually pertain to your actual life. You're always too wrapped up in theoretical bullshit."

"Killing the woman you've had a child with is a little different."

"Tell me how? How is it different?"

The Hitman grinned, feeling as if he had just checkmated his foe. "Why do I have to explain how killing your family is wrong? Are you that deranged that I have to explain the difference to you?" The Hitman was breathing heavy, trying not to lose his cool.

"Yes, please do. If we're all savage animals, why do you think what I did was wrong."

"When you put the ring on her finger, that's a vow that should never be broken. That's a vow saying that no matter what, you will protect each other. It says you have each others' backs no matter the cost, and you broke that," said The Hitman.

"Did she have my back when she was out fucking you? What vow of ours did she keep by sucking your cock? I never fucked around on her. I never even thought about it. She was my life before she decided she wanted to destroy it over some asshole. She was everything to me, and you took that away. You were the one she chose, not me. I placed a ring on her fucking finger, I gave up my life for her just so you could take her away from me? The bitch deserved to die," said The Pacifist.

"Even if you think that's true, you killed your own fucking child!" The Hitman slammed his hands on the table, spit flying furiously out of his mouth.

"She turned my own fucking child against me. Can you even imagine how that feels? Do you know how it feels when your own child comes up to you and tells you you're not a good father? She was growing up to be just like her mother and there was nothing I could do to stop it. I couldn't let my daughter do to another man what her mother did to me. I'd rather her be dead."

"You're a fucking animal. You deserve to be put down. You don't deserve life."

"I'm the one with the gun. I'm the bringer of death, not you."

"Until it doesn't go off, then you're forced to fork over your murder weapon to your fatal fate," The Hitman said.

"You're a killer, but you will not be the one who kills me," said The Pacifist.

"I'm afraid that's the case since there's no one else left to kill you but me."

"You can't kill someone who's already dead."

"Luckily your heart is still beating," The Hitman said. The buzzer went off. The Pacifist raised the gun and smiled, pointing it at The Hitman's forehead. He whispered a soft meditation chant as he pulled the trigger.

Russian Poker

-Click-

The Hitman

The Pacifist threw the gun at The Hitman as if he intended to hurt him with it. His pitch was perfectly aimed for The Hitman's open shoulder wound, but The Hitman caught it handily. The wound was still bleeding but it didn't slow down his reflexes any. The thought crossed The Pacifist's mind that he probably wasn't the first person to shoot The Hitman. "He's perfectly relaxed, and has taken the necessary medical precautions," The Pacifist whispered to himself. The Hitman pretended to ignore The Pacifist whispers while he loaded the bullet into the gun.

"This is it, you know? Three bullets are in the chamber. I don't think luck is on your side. This is where I kill you. This is where I get to walk out of here free. This is where I get my revenge," The Hitman said.

"This isn't revenge, this is finishing the fucking job. This is the final blow of you torturing me. You turned everyone I loved against me, then you needed to put me out of my fucking misery, didn't you?" The Pacifist cried. "This is what you want? To put me down like a fucking dog? Is that what I deserve? You've ruined my life, but that's not enough for you, is it? I've accepted my death, but I'll never accept my death at your hands. Anyone on the fucking planet but you. I'm not going to let you kill me. I'm simply not going to let it happen. I've already put one bullet into you, it'll be nothing to finish the job this time," The Pacifist said, clenching his eyes shut and rocking slightly back and forth.

"It's not your fucking choice whether you live or not. It's not your choice if I'm the one who does it. Do you think I feel any better about the man who killed the woman I love killing me?"

"She was my fucking wife."

"But I fucking loved her! You didn't love her. You didn't give a shit about her. You neglected one of the most beautiful and caring people in the world, then you killed her," The Hitman said.

"I loved her once. I spent half of my life with her. She cheated on you too. I caught her with another man. She was a whore. We had a family together. You and her didn't have shit. All you were to her was a fucking fling," The Pacifist replied.

"What? The reports never said anything about another man. It doesn't matter, I love her still, and you took it away from me. You took away my ability to ever love another woman again. You've ruined my life." The Hitman looked hurt by the news.

"I'm going to ruin it further by killing you."

"I know you're smart, and you know you're a coin flip decision away from being thrown in The Pile. Nothing you say to me is going to aggravate me enough to fire this gun before the buzzer goes off, and nothing is going to throw off my aim. I can land a fatal shot fifty yards away, but you couldn't even shoot and kill from three."

"If we both know this. Why not let me spend the few remaining minutes of life in silence?" The Pacifist said, giving a nod of acknowledgement to The Hitman. He nodded back in silent agreement. The Hitman tapped the barrel of the gun on table while The Pacifist appeared to meditate. The Hitman saw tears streaming down The Pacifist's face. He wasn't meditating, he was praying. The buzzer sounded, and The Pacifist clenched his eyes while a steady flow of tears poured out.

The Hitman aimed the gun at The Pacifist. "I...is there anything you'd like to say? Any last words to the world at large?"

"Yes, thank you," The Pacifist said opening his blood shot eyes at the camera. "I just want to say that this isn't the life I wanted to live. I always wanted to be a better person but didn't know how to do so until it was too late." He wiped the tears from his face and turned back to The Hitman. "I'm ready to accept my fate. Please do me the honor of putting me out of my misery and sending me on to my next journey."

-Bang-

The Story of Charles Turla

"After the war of your life, there is only peace"

Why don't I feel bad? I'm laying in the bed of a co-worker, and I don't feel the least bit bad about it. She came twice, then she sucked me off and there's not an ounce of remorse in me. Why not? Is it simply man's natural, biological inclination to procreate with multiple women, or do I just not care about the consequences? I should feel bad about this. It's immoral, but I don't care. Is it society that's wrong, or is there something wrong with me?

I still love her, I'm just not happy. Not that I'm happy with Stacey either. She just likes the thrill of fucking someone who's married. She's twenty-four years old, fresh out of college, and at her first job. She is the nerd I always wanted in a wife. Dark hair, thin, and appreciates Battlestar Galactica as much as I do. The kind of woman that looks worse without glasses. What is she even doing with me? I'd be cloddish to turn her down, but even that thought is immoral. How could it be immoral to not cheat on my wife?

Don't get me wrong, Stacey has her faults as well. She's deeply insecure. She's too afraid to look deep down to who she really is. She creates a facade decorated by labels to describe herself: musician, marathon runner, geek, animal rights activist, and vegetarian. She wraps titles around herself like wrapping paper, hoping no one tears them away, exposing who she really is.

"Hey hun, you all right?" Stacey says looking at me with her deep brown eyes.

"Yeah, I was just thinking. You know, about work stuff." She could tell I was lying, but she played along anyways.

"Yeah, you should not do that so much. C'mon, let's go and watch something. I'm pretty sure there's a Doctor Who marathon on right now," she says, nudging me with her elbow.

"I probably need to get going. It's my turn to cook tonight," I say. She always hates it when I mention anything having to do with my family. I can't say I blame her, but it's also the reason she's attracted to me.

"Yeah...that's fine." I could see the disappointment on her face. She wants me to stay. She really wants to be with me. Even though we've talked about it, she still thinks this will be a relationship. In a way, it is. We've been having this affair for nine months. I've cheated on my wife dozens of times and not once did I feel bad.

"Oh, cheer up. How about we go to the museum on Saturday? They opened up a new exhibit last month." I could never drag my wife to museums, plays, or anything remotely intellectually stimulating. What did I see in her other than being nothing like any other girl I ever dated? I blame it on being young and being tired of dating girls identical to me. Maybe I just don't like people like me, but I like Stacey, so who knows?

"Yeah, that sounds good. You better get back to your family."

"You busy on Thursday?" I ask as she sighs.

"You know Thursday is my Zumba night, and there's no way I'm letting you see me that sweaty."

"Oh damn, that's right. Well, we will figure something out before the weekend, okay?" I pat her on the head and roll out of bed. I make sure I tuck my shirt in and get my tie perfect. I don't need her suspecting anything. I give Stacey a kiss. Still nothing, not an ounce of remorse. I kiss her again and her lips open. I slide my tongue in her mouth. No remorse. I pull away.

On my way home I think about a plethora of things. The morality of cheating, why men cheat, and why women care so little as long as we go home to them. I don't come to any conclusions. I don't think I ever will either. Until my brain can logically decipher any reason not to do it, I know I won't stop. If it wasn't Stacey, I'd just find someone else.

I better pick up some wine for tonight. I'd like to have a nice dinner with my wife for once. I stop at the liquor store a few blocks away and pick up a bottle of Caduceus Merkin. It's a 2006 reserve, I believe. No matter how much extravagant wine I let her taste, she never likes it. You just can't teach someone to have a good palate. I pull into the driveway. One of these days I'll call the repair man to fix the garage door. Until that day, it'll be the home for what she passes as art these days.

I step out of the car and close the door. I hit the button, locking the doors. I always seem to forget to do so, or I'll accidentally hit the panic button instead. Who uses that button intentionally anyway? I keep my keys in my hand as I go to the front door. I turn the key in the knob and hear the lock click open. I twist the handle, shoving the door open with my shoulder.

I immediately notice the house smells like a bakery. It's doubtful she's cooking, and much more likely that she's burning a candle in the kitchen. As suspected, I find a candle burning that's supposed to smell like mint brownies as I walk into the kitchen. Mint is my favorite scent. There's just something satisfying about how refreshing, and yet how still sweet it is. I put the wine on the counter and lay my keys beside it.

I hear her rapidly coming down the stairs. "Jeez, you trying to break the world record or something?" I yell at her before I even see her.

"No, nothing like that. I'm just excited to see you, of course" she says. Something isn't right here. There's a sense of urgency in her voice. "How was work?" She asks standing at the bottom of the stairs.

"It was superb as always. James needed me to stay late to wrap up this account that they made a total wreck out of. You know how I just can't leave work until something like that is done," I say.

"Oh yeah I do. So you want to cook tonight or should we order in? I don't feel like cooking tonight," she says still at the bottom of the stairs. She never makes excuses for not wanting to cook. Something more is definitely going on.

"I'll cook. I had an idea today at lunch for a dessert egg roll. Let me go ahead and change first, then I'll get started," I say as I unbutton my cuffs and take off my shoes.

"W-why not just, you know, cook in what your wearing?" She says. She's nervous...how predictable. She may be a smart woman, but she's definitely not clever.

"Because these are my work clothes and you know I'm a messy cook." I need to go upstairs. She's obviously hiding something. She spreads her arms across the stairwell, still standing on the bottom step.

"Please don't go up there" she says.

"What the fuck are you hiding from me? I swear to God, you better get out of the way or you'll regret it," I say, moving towards her. I grab her wrists as she continues to block the way. She resists. Why would she resist unless she really thinks she's stronger than me? "Do you think I'm some sort of pussy? What the fuck is wrong with you?" I twist her wrist, and then yank her arm towards me. The rest of her body follows. "Stupid bitch." I go upstairs.

"No, please don't," she says, sobbing behind me. I can

feel her trying to grab at my feet. I ignore her attempts. I go into our bedroom. The bed is made better than it usually is. The lamp is on. She never leaves the lamp on. There's something next to it...a condom wrapper? Fuck. I open the closet....nothing. I check under the bed...nothing there either.

I step back into the hallway and into my daughter's bedroom. There's no way he's fucking hiding in my daughter's room while she's sleeping. The door creaks as I open it. My daughter's sound asleep in her crib. I tip toe around the room, ready to rip the fucker's heart out. This is my child. I hear her snore lightly. There's something adorable about hearing babies snore and I don't quite understand why. I check the closet...nothing. There's no way he could hide under her crib. I head back into the hallway.

I'm pushed to the ground from behind. There's a man on top of me. He hits me with an elbow across my head. I feel my forehead splitting open. I turn to my side and quickly stand up. He's white, short and hefty. This is what my wife has been fucking? I guess six years of kick boxing is going to come of good use.

I punch him in the face with a left jab, and follow up with a right hook. He winces as I drive the palm of my hand into his nose. I feel the cartilage breaking, and see the blood flowing from his nose. He raises his hand up to his nose to wipe the blood away. I grab the back of his neck with both hands and ram it into my knee as I raise it. With his body doubled over, I drive my elbow into the base of his neck. He falls to the ground with a grunt. The way his head is laying makes me think his neck is broken. I stomp on his neck with all my weight, and it squishes under my foot. I hear my wife, Danielle, come up the stairs.

She is crying hysterically. "Honey, I think we should talk," I say before she reaches the top step. She screams as soon as she sees the body under my feet.

"Calm the fuck down! Our child is still fucking sleeping," I say.

"What the fuck are you doing?" she says walking over to the body of whoever it was she was just fucking and I just murdered.

"What am I doing? What the fuck are you doing? Honey, I think we need to talk," I say.

"What do you mean? Please, please don't hurt me," she pleads with me.

"Hurt you? So now you're concerned about hurting me? Were you concerned about it when you were fucking him? I'm not going to have anyone take my place. This is all mine. You're taking my life away from me! I've given you everything, and you've shit all over me. What have I ever done to you? Is this what I deserve? You fuck him in my bed I paid for. You didn't pay for shit, and you still suck his dick on the bed that I paid for. Am I that terrible, or are you that much of a whore?" I ask.

"No, please no," she cries.

"Is it because he's more attractive than me? Is that it? Does he have a bigger dick? Is that why you fucked around on me? Huh, is it? Is it? He's not so attractive now, is he? You want his dick? Go on and suck it now, you bitch! How much do you want his ass now? Just tell me, what did I ever do to you?"

"You're never there for me. You're never here for me when I need you. You're always preoccupied with your job. You gave up on me. I never gave up on you."

"I never cheated on you! You fucked around on me. I never gave up on you," I say.

"And you think you're some sort of saint? You think I wanted to cheat on you? I love you, but you've ignored me for years. What did you expect me to do? It's been months since we've fucked. What changed? Why is it you don't want anything to do with me anymore? Am I ugly? Have I gotten fat? Why won't you just tell me what it is?" Danielle says.

"You quit being you," I reply. "There was a single moment, I remember, I came home and you bitched at me because I left my socks under the coffee table. The day before that, you didn't care, but you changed that day for some reason, and you never came back. You became someone who I loved but I felt like I didn't know anymore. I felt it on that day when I looked into your eyes and no longer saw the woman who loves me, but saw the woman who wanted nothing more than to bitch at me. For the first time, I saw a woman who no longer cared about me."

"Your socks always bothered me. I just never said anything until I couldn't take it anymore. I was going to let you try to grow up on your own, but it's obvious that wasn't going to happen. I just wanted you to be an adult. Is that so much to ask?" She cries.

"That's the problem with women, you think you have things figured out. Only thing is you don't realize how much dumber you are than men. Guess how the world works? If you have a problem, you tell it to me so I can fix it. Instead women hide and don't tell us the shit that's bothering you until you get so fed up, you suck someone other than your husband's dick. Sound familiar? That's not my fault, that's yours," I yell at her. "But that doesn't really matter now, does it? What are we going to do now? I'm not going to jail. I'd rather die than go to jail. So what are we going to do?" I say.

"I...I don't know. I don't know how to get rid of a body," she says taking a step closer to me.

"But what other option do we have?" I say to her while placing my hand on her shoulder. "This is what we have to deal with." I lower my head and close my eyes to concentrate.

"What about Prairie Dog River?" She suggest with tears

in her eyes. "They dump bodies there all the time."

"I can't do this. I don't want this. I just want everything to be okay," I say to myself.

"Honey, are you okay? You're breathing really heavy," she says, and she's right. I didn't realize it, but the adrenaline of killing someone must have me hyperventilating. The more I try to calm my breathing, the harder it becomes to do so. My vision begins to blur, and I clench my teeth. My mind wanders to what's going to happen to me when I'm in prison. I can't go, I just can't! There has to be a way out of all of this.

Someone touches my shoulder, and I bat it away. They're trying to take me away. They're trying to take everything away from me. I run blindly to my daughter's room. I won't let them take her from me. I go to her crib...it's empty. They already got to her. I drop to my knees and sob. I can't handle this. I can't do this. They already took her from me.

I put my hands over my head and dig my fingernails into my scalp. I clench until I feel blood seep through my fingers. I feel the skin start to tear away from my skull. I hear a voice come from the darkness.

"Honey, are you okay? You're having a panic attack again. Shh, it's okay baby," the unfamiliar voice says. I can't breathe. My lungs feel frozen, and I swear it's spreading. I need to get out of here before they find me. I dash out of my daughter's room and into the hallway. There's someone blocking my path at the top of the stairs. I don't stop. I plow through the figure. We both tumble down the stairs. I hear the bones cracking underneath me when we land at the bottom. The body underneath me stiffens. I roll off the body and head toward the front door.

I turn around, making sure no one is following me. The body at the bottom of the stairs is completely lifeless. The image is still blurry, and my head is pounding. My heart feels like it's going to seize up and stop pumping blood at any moment. My vision is going black. I stumble towards the door, and fall down. I stop breathing, and everything is going black. I'm dying.

When I wake up, my head throbs so bad that I'm still disoriented. The house is quiet. I sit up and pull my IPhone out of my pocket to see what time it is. There's a text from Stacey. It says she can't do it anymore, and that she feels guilty about being the other woman. She says she's sorry about leading me on, thinking that she was okay with it when she wasn't. A second message from Stacey pops up and tells me that I should enjoy a life with my wife and child, and that should be enough to make me happy.

I am light headed and dizzy as I stand up. I regain my balance and walk towards the stairs. I don't see any assailant trying to take me away. All I see is my wife at the bottom of the stairs with both hands clutching a blanket. I walk over and pry her hand away from the blanket...no pulse. I tug on the blanket to see what's underneath it that she needed to cling to so dearly. It's my daughter.

Neither of them move. My daughter is as lifeless as my wife. I look at my phone and my fingers are trembling. What the fuck did do? How can I live with myself? I dial 9-1-1. I tell the dispatcher what I have done. I tell the dispatcher that I'll be waiting for the police to arrest me in the garden. I hang up and walk outside.

The garden is the only place me and my wife actually interacted, albeit only for a few hours every weekend. I step over to the bed of iris flowers. She won't see the irises grow this year. Purple was her favorite color. That's why she wanted a whole bed of irises. She'll never see them. One of the bulbs is half sticking out of the ground. I dig it up and hold it in my hands.

I don't know how long I was on my knees with a bulb in my hand, but I heard voices and knew this was almost over. I see the reflection of the blue and red lights from of the bulb in my hand. I hear whispers behind me, but I ignore them. I enjoy the last few moments of my freedom until I serve my lifetime of hell. A hell that I deserve. I'm sorry for all the wrong I've done in my life. I just wish I could have been as beautiful and pure as this bed of flowers.

Epilogue

As expected, ~~The~~ his aim was impeccable. The bullet entered The Pacifist's body in the middle of his forehead and lodged halfway through his brain. A small trickle of blood dripped down the back of his head and puddled onto the floor beneath him. He stood up, tucking the pistol in the back of his pants, and waited for the door to open. Ten minutes later, three people entered the room. The Short Guard and The Tall Guard were accompanied by The Warden.

The Tall Guard immediately grabbed the body of The Pacifist from behind and dragged him out of the room. Blood gushed from The Pacifist's forehead, soaking through The Tall Guard's pants. The Tall Guard cursed loudly. The Short Guard stood with The Warden by the door. The Warden pulled a pistol from the back of his pants and aimed it at him. His heart dropped, realizing he didn't win after all. He was just the last to lose.

The Warden spoke. "Congratulations kid. Come with me." He followed The Warden, stepping out of the room, and out of his death sentence. "We have some business to take care of," The Warden said. He felt the barrel of a pistol against his back. Every step he took he expected it to go off. He thought they might be taking him to the shower for an easy clean-up, or worse yet, The Pile. They walked past the cell block where he had lived and continued further down the corridor.

The corridor seemed endless. Cell after cell, door after door, it all looked the same. Except one room, the last room on the left. That door led into the minimum security checkpoint. That door was open. The Tall Guard stepped through the door and into the room, dragging The Pacifist with him. He immediately knew exactly why the door was left open. It was The Pile. His stomach turned at the thought. They got to the security checkpoint where The Short Guard pushed him into a room, shutting the door behind them.

The one dim light in the room was more than enough to illuminate The Pile. It was worse than he had imagined. It wasn't just a pile of bodies, it was a tangled mess of mangled carcasses. The blood of the losers mixed together like a cocktail. It wasn't individual people who he had known, it was its own entity, it was The Pile. He could see limbs come out of every direction, several with bones protruding from the skin. There was a flap of skin pulled back from The Woman's head, exposing her skull. There wasn't any order to it, just bodies haphazardly tossed on top of each other. He expected The Pile to come alive at any moment like a zombie Frankenstein.

He contemplated whether this was some sort of joke or if this was where he was going to live now. He searched around the room, looking for a way out. There was a vent near the floor on other side of The Pile. The Pile occupied the majority of the room. He would have to sneak around it, hoping not to get more gore on him. Someone grabbed his leg. As he looked down, the hand of The Preacher was around his ankle. The Hitman kicked it away and continued around the room, and around The Pile. He crept to the vent. It was screwed in tight. He jammed a fingernail into one of the screws and twisted it.

"You going somewhere?" a voice asked.

"Seems like you're always fighting to be free," he said. "Well c'mon, we're waitin' on ya. Try not to fuck any of the bodies on your way out unless you like sloppy seconds," the voice said. He didn't plan on making the voice on the other side of the door wait any longer than necessary. He walked around the The Pile and stepped through the door. The Tall Guard met him on the other side. "Did you have fun playing with your old friends?" he asked. "Why did you put me in there?" He asked. He was three shades lighter than before he entered the room.

"We had to keep you occupied while we took care of some paperwork. He's ready to see you now. Come this way," The Tall Guard said. There were no handcuffs this time, no walking down a hall with a gun pressed into his back. He was following The Tall Guard through several twists and turns, stairwells and security check points. Not a word was spoken between them as they arrived at The Warden's office. The Tall Guard simply opened the door, and shut it behind him once he entered.

The room was cozier than he expected. It had a full

length leather couch against the wall with a bar cabinet to the side of an oak bookshelf with a random assortment of books. The only one he recognized from the cover was To Kill a Mockingbird.

"First of all, congratulations. That was pretty impressive," The Warden said.

"Thanks. I did what was needed to win," he replied.

"Indeed you did." The Warden folded his hands over his solid oak desk. "Here's the deal. We can let you go right now with fifteen thousand dollars cash in your pocket. You will have no protection from us. I can not promise you'll make it five feet without the mob outside making a mini-pile out of you. If you make it out through that, you'll struggle for the rest of your life just even going to get gas without being called a murderer. Not to mention your former employer may want to have some choice words with you."

"Or?" he asked, knowing this wasn't going to be a single offer situation.

"Or...we offer you a job," The Warden said

"What kind of job?"

"I can't tell you the duties of the job until you agree to do it," The Warden said.

"What should I expect if I walk out?" He asked.

"You'll be a superstar more than likely. Television interviews, book deals, hell, maybe even a movie. You'll be the most famous person everyone wants dead. You'll lead a good life if no one tries to kill you."

"And if I take the job?"

"Then you're an employed citizen."

"Employed by who?"

"If you want to know, sign the paper." The Warden pulled out two plain manilla envelopes from a drawer in his desk. He opened the first one and placed it to his left. While he read over the print of the first contract, The Warden opened the second envelope and placed it to his right. He looks over the the second contract, reading every word carefully.

"So two years, two million each year, then what?" he said after he finished reading the contracts.

"If you succeed, you live your life as you want. By that time no one is going to

care who you are," The Warden said.

"And if I don't succeed?" He asked.

"I think you know the answer to that. This wasn't just a game, it was an interview. We were contracted by the employer to get the most savage, ruthless killer we could find for a special mission. The company would like to hire someone in your position, and they only wanted the best. That's why we made you play the game. We would have much rather just executed all you bastards, but truth be told, the state is making a shit ton of money off the deal as well. That's not even including the money from the ratings. No one wants you to live, but you've been given a chance. What are you going to do?" The Warden asked, leaning forward in his chair.

He thought about how rare moments like this happen in his life, moments where his life was branching into two distinct paths. He would have to make a choice of which path to take. He knew what he wanted to do but he didn't know how to prepare himself for it. He didn't know what to expect when he signed the contract. He's lived life being prepared for everything, but nothing could prepare him for what he was about to do.

"So have you made your decision?" He looked up at The Warden and nodded. "Good. Sign the contract and we'll get everything ready." The Warden offered him a pen to sign the contract. The only thing left for him to do was to sign his life away. He picked a contract and signed. "I know you've been through a lot, but it's over now," The Warden said. He gathered the unsigned contract and placed it in a nearby paper shredder.

"There's no turning back now," The Warden said while opening the door. "Anything else you'd like to say before this gets underway?"

"I just want to thank you for the opportunity for giving me life," he said as he offered The Warden his hand. The Warden's handshake was as heavy handed as he thought it would be. He smiled to himself at the predictability. "So what's next?"

"You've been on the clock from the second you signed the contract. Your employer will be here shortly. Be the best killer you can, and you'll do just fine. Oh and kid, congratulations. You earned it"

25972087R00206

Made in the USA
Charleston, SC
17 January 2014